Classic
Tales from India
How Ganesh Got His Elephant Head
and Other Stories

VATSALA SPERLING & HARISH JOHARI

ILLUSTRATED BY PIETER WELTEVREDE,

NONA WELTEVREDE, AND SANDEEP JOHARI

Bear Cub Books
Rochester, Vermont

For Dada, Harish Johari

Bear Cub Books
One Park Street
Rochester, Vermont 05767
www.InnerTraditions.com

Bear Cub Books is a division of Inner Traditions International

Cataloging-in-Publication Data for this title is available from the Library of Congress

ISBN 978-1-59143-386-6 (print)
ISBN 978-1-59143-387-3 (ebook)

Printed and bound in India by Replika Press Pvt. Ltd.

10 9 8 7 6 5 4 3 2

Text design and layout by Virginia Scott Bowman
This book was typeset in Berkeley Oldstyle with Abbess, Apple Chancery, Metamorphous, and Nueva used as display typefaces

To send correspondence to the author of this book, mail a first-class letter to the author c/o Inner Traditions • Bear & Company, One Park Street, Rochester, VT 05767, and we will forward the communication.

Introduction

Dear Readers,

You will be delighted to know that India is famous not just for its Bollywood movies, snake charmers, peacocks, basmati rice, and super-spicy curry—it is also famous for the stories from its ancient mythology, which are filled with colorful, brave, and mysterious characters. Hindu cosmology divides time into four *yugas*, or eras—the Sat yuga, Treta yuga, Dwapara yuga, and Kali yuga. Each yuga sees a gradual decline of virtue, wisdom, intellect, and strength in humankind. We are currently living in the Kali yuga. The incidents described in Indian mythology took place during the earlier yugas of India's distant past, when gods, demons, humans, wise men, maharishis, and animals walked on Earth with ease and, with equal ease, could shape-shift from one form of being to another. All of these beings could also have children with one another, resulting in progeny who were half human–half god, half human–half demon, half god–half demon, or a host of other combinations. And each of the groups on Earth could converse with the others using a common language that all of them understood. These stories of India's ancient past have left an indelible mark on the mind of every Indian citizen.

Even today, millions of Indians name their children after the gods and goddesses of Indian mythology, giving them names such as Ganesh, Shiva, Vishnu, Ram, Krishna, Lakshmi, Parvati, or Saraswati. And to this day, these gods and goddesses are worshipped in homes and temples all across the length and breadth of India. Similarly, there are many, many Indian towns, cities, and villages that get their names from locations described in Indian mythology, such as Ayodhya, Vrindavan, Varanasi, Indraprastha, and Mathura. Though some may believe that the mythological stories of India are based on someone's rich imagination, her mythology is, in fact, her history. And this rich history has shaped the culture, social norms, religion, and language of the country. But because this history is so, so, so ancient, and the events took place so many, many, many thousands of years ago, these events are considered "stories" today.

As long as I lived in India (where I was born and raised) it was easy for me to remain immersed in these mythological stories. And then, when I moved to the United States to start a family, I was very pleasantly surprised to find that Westerners were quite intrigued by Indian deities such as Ganesh, Shiva, and Ganga. They could often figure out that I was a Hindu from India, which prompted them to ask me many, many questions about the gods and goddesses worshipped in my country. In supermarkets and farmers' markets, in gas stations and bus stations, in libraries and schools, and in airplanes and trains, these curious people presented their questions to me. If I were to make a list of all their questions, I would need several pages. This unique experience of fielding questions from complete strangers prompted me to write stories for American children about the mythological characters of my homeland.

For this work, I studied the sacred epics such as the Mahabharata and the Ramayana, and shorter texts including the *Bhagavad Gita, Srimad Bhagavatam, Shiva Purana,* and *Vishnu Purana.* I also realized that all the stories that my mother had told me in my childhood were still fresh in my mind. My mother, Mrs. Narayani Ramnath, had a prodigious and photographic memory for the historical and mythological texts and epics of India. And she could remember them in three languages—Sanskrit, Tamil, and Hindi! During my childhood we didn't have television, radio, cell phones, or computers in our home. After school my four older sisters, my older brother, and I did our homework quickly, ate our supper very quickly, and then gathered every evening around our mother for our story time. As a storyteller par excellence, she regaled us for hours every evening. She was our one and only source of entertainment. Sometimes she read books to us. At other times she sang large portions of the epics in her sweet and melodious voice. And as an accomplished singer of Karnatic music, she also composed lyrics and created devotional music of her own to honor various gods and goddesses. She sang these as well, and we sang along with her.

After telling us the ancient stories of our heritage, she would encourage us to express our point of view and take home messages from any character whom we liked or disliked. She never told us what to think because she wanted us to draw our own conclusions and learn the spiritual, social, cultural, ethical, and practical lessons we needed to learn from the mythological characters. I still recall fondly those evenings spent on my mother's lap listening to stories, and for this unique, electronics-free time, I am profoundly grateful to my first teacher, my mother. Having learned these stories at her knee, I found that the inspiration for writing new versions of the stories—in English for a new American audience—came naturally to me.

I have added a note to parents and teachers at the end of every story in this volume, in which I examine and discuss significant aspects of the main characters. Each of these stories from India encourages us to seek truth and higher ideals. By example, the characters from Indian mythology tell us how to distinguish between right and wrong, generosity and selfishness, forgiveness and revenge, fear and bravery, weakness and power, self-serving demands and prayer, seriousness and playfulness, laziness and industriousness, distraction and focus. When we—or our children—read these stories with care and attention to the depth and wisdom of the characters, our own tendencies and character improve too, and we become better people. These mythological stories from India also convey the essence of India as expressed in the phrases *Vasudhaiva kutumbakam,* "The whole world is a family," and *Satyameva jayate,* "Only truth wins."

I have written these stories for the present and future of children all over the world, and I dedicate this book to children with much love.

Thank you,

Vatsala Sperling, PhD, PDHom, CCH, RSHom

Contents
and
Cast of Characters

The following five characters appear in many of the stories that follow.

Brahma
(Brahm-'ha)
God of Creation

Shiva
('Sheev-a)
God of Destruction

Vishnu
('Vish-noo)
God of Preservation

Indra
('In-dra)
God of Thunder and Lightning, the
king of the lesser gods

Narada
('Nah-rah-da)
Wise sage who could travel between
Heaven, Earth, and the Underworld
at the speed of light

How Ganesh Got His Elephant Head • page 15

Parvati ('Par-va-tee)

A great mother goddess, wife of Shiva, mother of Ganesh and Kartikeya

Shivaganas (Shee-va-g'-'nas)

Shiva's assistants, a band of troublemakers

Nandi (Nahn-dee)

Shiva's pet bull

Kartikeya (Kar-ti-'kay-a)

Brother of Ganesh, commander in chief of Indra's army

Garuda (Gar-oo-'da)

Vishnu's pet eagle

Nav Durga (Nahv 'Door-ga)

A fierce goddess who appears in nine forms and protects the innocent against injustice

Kali (Kah-lee)

Goddess of Destruction

Ganesh (G'-nesh)

The elephant-headed god who can make things go right, son of Parvati and Shiva

How Parvati Won the Heart of Shiva • page 43

Mena ('May-na)

Wife of Himalaya, mother of Parvati

Himalaya (Hi-ma-lay-'a)

King of the Mountains, husband of Mena, father of Parvati

Adishakti ('A-dee-'shak-tee)

The great mother goddess, Shiva's wife in Heaven

Kama ('Ka-ma)

The god of earthly love and desire

Rati (Ra-'tee)

Wife of Kama

Parvati ('Par-va-tee)

An earthly form of Adishakti, Shiva's betrothed on Earth

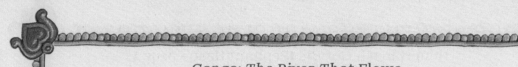

Ganga: The River That Flows from Heaven to Earth • page 71

Bali ('Baah-lee)

A virtuous demon king who banished the lazy gods from Heaven

Kashyapa and Aditi (Kahsh-ya-pa) ('Aah-dee-tee)

A virtuous sage and his wife, Lord Vishnu's earthly parents

Vamana ('Vaah-ma-na)

Lord Vishnu's incarnation on Earth as a dwarf

Shukracharya (Shuk-'raah-'chaar-ya)

A sage who is the teacher of demons

Ganga (Gan-'ga)

Daughter of Lord Brahma, a river that came from Heaven to Earth

Durvasa (Dur-'vaah-'saah)

A sage well known for his anger and terrible curses

Sagar ('Saah-gar)

A king with sixty thousand sons who wanted to rule the whole universe

Kapil (Ka-pil)

A sage who was falsely accused of stealing King Sagar's horse

Anshuman (An-shu-man)

King Sagar's only surviving son

Bhagirath (Bha-'ghee-raht-h)

A descendant of King Sagar whose devotion brought Ganga to Earth as a sacred river

Jahnu ('Jaah-nu)

A sage who drank up the entire River Ganga

Ram (Rahm)
Incarnation of Lord
Vishnu on Earth,
son of Dasharatha,
husband of Sita

**Lakshman
('Lahk-sh-mahn)**
Ram's brother, incarnation
of Lord Vishnu's serpent,
Shesha

**Bharat and Shatrughna
('Bha-raht)
('Shaht-ru-gh-na)**
Ram's younger brothers,
incarnations of the conch
and mace of Lord Vishnu

Sita ('See-tah)
Incarnation of Goddess
Lakshmi on Earth, daughter
of King Janaka, Ram's wife

Dasharatha (Da-'sh-ra-ta)
King of Ayodhya, father
of Ram

**Hanuman
(Han-oo-'mahn)**
Son of the wind god, Pavan

Janaka (Juh-'nuhk)
King of Mithila,
father of Sita

Vasistha (Vah-'shis-ta)
Royal counselor of
King Dasharatha

Ravana ('Rah-va-'nah)
Demon with ten heads,
King of Lanka

**Maricha and Subahu
('Mar-i-ch) (Su-bah-'hoo)**
Demons who make
mischief

Manthara (Mun-t-'rah)
Queen Kaikeyi's
wicked maid

**Jambavan
(Jahm-bah-'vahn)**
Lord Brahma's son,
King of the Bears

**Shurpanakha
('Shoor-pah-nah-kha)**
Sister of Ravana

**Kumbhakarna
(Kuhmb-'ha-khar-na)**
Demon who slept for six
months at a stretch,
brother of Ravana

Tataka ('Tah-ta-kah)
Demon of the dead forest

Hanuman's Journey
to the Medicine Mountain • page 131

Hanuman
(Han-oo-'mahn)
Son of the wind god, Pavan;
minister of Sugriva;
devotee of Ram

Sugriva
(Soo-'gree-va)
Deposed King
of the Monkeys

Sampati
('Sam-pa-tee)
King of the Vultures,
brother of Jatayu

Surasa
('Soor-a-sa)
A demon guarding
the ocean

Vibhishana
(Vib-'heesh-a-na)
Ravana's younger brother,
devotee of Lord Vishnu

Indrajeet
('In-dra-jeet)
Son of Ravana

Note: Many of the characters in *Hanuman's Journey to the Medicine Mountain*
appear in *Ram the Demon Slayer*. (See previous page.)

The Magical Adventures
of Krishna • page 161

Lakshmi
('Lack-shmee)
Lord Vishnu's wife,
Goddess of Wealth

Shesha
('Shay-sha)
Lord Vishnu's
serpent

Krishna
('Krish-nah)
Incarnation of Lord Vishnu
on Earth; his name means
"midnight-blue"

Radha
('Raad-'haa)
Krishna's girlfriend,
incarnation of Goddess
Lakshmi on Earth

Balaram
('Bala-rahm)
Krishna's cousin,
incarnation of
Shesha on Earth

Bhumi
('Boo-mee)
The earth goddess
who appears as a cow

Kansa
('Kahn-sa)
King of Mathura,
Krishna's uncle

Yogamaya
(Yohg-'my-a)
Goddess of Illusion,
appears as the fierce
goddess Durga

Devaki
(Day-vah-'kee)
King Kansa's sister,
Krishna's mother

Vasudeva
(Vah-soo-'day-vah)
Devaki's husband,
Krishna's father

Yashoda
(Yah-'sho-da)
Krishna's adoptive
mother

Trinavarta
(Trin-'ah-vra-ta)
A demon who appears
as a whirlwind

Vatasura
(Vah-'tah-soor-a)
A demon who
appears as a calf

Bakasura
(Bock-'ah-soor-a)
A demon who
appears as a bird

Aghasura
(Agh-'ha-soor-a)
A demon who
appears as a serpent

Akrura
(Ah-'kroor-a)
A wise devotee of
Lord Vishnu

Who Is the Greatest Archer in the World: Karna or Arjuna? • page 191

Kunti
(Kun-'tee)

Birth mother of Karna,
wife of King Pandu,
mother of the first
three Pandava brothers

Madri
('Maa-dree)

Second wife of King
Pandu and mother to
the last two Pandava
brothers

Arjuna
(Ar-'joo-na)

Son given to Kunti
by Lord Indra

Karna
(Kar-'naah)

Son born to Princess
Kunti and the Sun God,
adopted by Adhiratha
and Radha

Dhritrashtra
(Dhrit-'raah-strah)

King Pandu's blind
older brother, father
of Duryodhana

Gandhari
('Gaahn-'dhaa-ree)

Wife of Dhritrashtra,
mother of Duryodhana;
she wears a blindfold
to empathize with her
blind husband

Duryodhana
(Dur-'yoh-dhan-a)

Firstborn son of
Dhritrashtra and
Gandhari, greedy
cousin of the Pandava
brothers

Shakuni
(Sha-ku-'nee)

Duryodhana's crafty
uncle, Gandhari's
brother

Bhishma
('Bhish-maa)

Wise grandfather of
Pandu, Dhritrashtra,
and Vidur; son of
Goddess Ganga and
King Shantanu

Vidur
(Vi-dur)

Wise uncle of the
Pandava brothers as
well as Duryodhana
and his ninety-nine
brothers and one sister

Drona
(Dro-naa)

Royal teacher of
the Pandavas and
Duryodhana and his
ninety-nine brothers

Draupadi
(Drow-pa-'dee)

Wife of the Pandava
brothers

Krishna
('Krish-na)
Lord Vishnu, born on Earth
as Queen Kunti's nephew,
cousin of the Pandava
brothers

Indra
('In-dra)
God of Thunder and
Lightning, disguised
as a Brahmin

Durvasa
(Dur-'vaah-'saah)
A sage who gives
Kunti a secret mantra
for calling the gods

Adhiratha
(Ad-hi-raht-'haah)
Karna's adoptive father,
husband of Radha

Radha
(Rah-'dhaah)
Karna's adoptive mother,
wife of Adhiratha

Pandu
('Paahn-doo)
King of Hastinapur,
husband of Kunti
and Madri, father of
the Pandava brothers

Sage Parasuram
(Parah-shu-r'aahm)
The sage who
teaches archery to Karna

The Pandava ('Paahn-da-va) brothers
Yudhisthira (Yudh-'eesh-tira), Bhima ('Bhee-ma),
and **Arjuna (Ar-'joo-na)** are sons of Pandu and
Kunti, **Nakula ('Nah-koo-la)** and **Sahadeva
(Sa-'ha-day-vah)** are sons of Pandu and Madri. All
five boys are gifts from the gods, so they are
half human and half god

How Ganesh Got His Elephant Head

Harish Johari and Vatsala Sperling

Illustrated by Pieter Weltevrede

How Ganesh Got
His Elephant Head

About Ganesh

This is the story of Ganesh, a very odd-looking and wonderful god. If you were to visit India, you would be sure to see countless little roadside temples built for him in every village and town. And in those temples you would find bowls of sugarcane, fruit, milk, peanuts, and coconuts-and, perhaps, some nice, freshly cut hay! For Ganesh has the body of a chubby little boy but the head of a baby elephant, and people like to give him the goodies that baby elephants love the best.

Ganesh is known as the god who removes obstacles. Many Hindus ask for his blessing before beginning any undertaking, be it something as big as getting married, or something as small as planting a single seed. Ganesh makes wishes come true-if they are good wishes-and helps people find a way around their difficulties.

Ganesh is a friendly little god who is loved as much as he is worshipped. He is appealing, humble, and even comical. Instead of riding on a bird of prey or some monstrous beast, he rides a little mouse. Like Ganesh himself, the lowly, nibbling mouse knows no obstacles. Together they go anywhere they need to.

Hindus see Ganesh as the god who has the power to make all good things happen. He inspires people to love one another, to play beautiful music, paint marvelous pictures, or write really good books. And if anyone is fighting an injustice or struggling with someone who is unfair, that person can depend on Ganesh. With his help, justice prevails, and right wins out over wrong.

You are probably wondering how in the world a little boy wound up with the head of a baby elephant, and what in the world gives him so much power to make things go right. Like Ganesh himself, the story is strange and wonderful. Listen carefully, and I'll tell it to you.

Shiva, God of Destruction, was married to the beautiful mother goddess Parvati, who had come to Earth in the form of a mountain princess. He loved his wife deeply and passionately, but he cared nothing for the schedules or dress codes or manners of a royal household. Clad in a tiger skin, with live serpents coiled around his waist and shoulders, a crescent moon on his brow, and long matted hair down his back, he roamed the wilderness for weeks at a time, with no one but animals for company.

In spite of his unruly ways, Parvati loved Shiva just the way he was. The only time she protested his behavior was when he arrived in her private chambers without warning and interrupted her in her bath.

One afternoon Parvati lay soaking in a warm tub. Shiva had been gone for weeks. When would she see him next? Would he burst through the door right then and there? The thought of him barging in so rudely troubled Parvati and made it hard for her to relax.

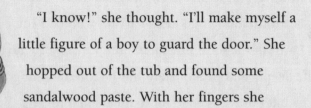

"I know!" she thought. "I'll make myself a little figure of a boy to guard the door." She hopped out of the tub and found some sandalwood paste. With her fingers she fashioned a head, a cute button nose, and two big eyes. Working quickly, she created sturdy legs and arms. The figurine looked quite lifelike!

She took a breath and blew life into it.

Suddenly, a little boy sprang forth, as strong and handsome as could be. He jumped lightly to the floor and turned to face her.

"Dear Mother," the boy said, "now that I am here, what can I do for you?"

"Dear Son, please just stand at the palace door while I finish my bath, and do not let anyone in." She gave him a slender wand to hold. "Here," she said with a smile. "Just wave this at anyone who tries to enter."

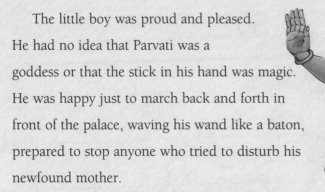

The little boy was proud and pleased.
He had no idea that Parvati was a
goddess or that the stick in his hand was magic.
He was happy just to march back and forth in
front of the palace, waving his wand like a baton,
prepared to stop anyone who tried to disturb his
newfound mother.

And so when Shiva, true to form,
strode up to the palace door, he
found a sturdy youngster with a
strong voice and determined
eyes barring his way.
"Entry denied, sir!"
said the boy.

Shiva was puzzled. Who was this child? And
why was he, Lord Shiva, God of Destruction,
experiencing such difficulty getting past
him? Shiva found that he couldn't
take a single step forward! There was
some strange, powerful force holding him back.
As usual, though, Shiva was in a hurry to return to
the forest, so he asked his pet bull, Nandi, to
investigate for him.

The bull, backed up by Shiva's helpers, a band of ruffians called the Shivaganas, lowered his long horns to attack. But the brave little boy waved his wand, once, twice, three times—and before they knew it, Nandi and his cohorts were in full retreat. They were mortified. This was the very first time anyone had dared stand up to them. And worse yet, they had been defeated by a pudgy little boy!

They found Shiva walking in the forest. "I'm sorry, Lord Shiva," Nandi said, hanging his great head in shame. "The boy just waved his wand! We could not go forward. It must have been very powerful magic!"

Far away, the sage Narada—an amazing and wise spirit who traveled between Heaven and Earth and the netherworlds below—heard every word. Narada kept careful watch on all goings on in the universe, and he could carry news of events and problems at the speed of light. The way he told the news made everyone pay attention too! When Narada got involved, you could be sure that things would really start happening.

When he saw the boy drive all intruders from Parvati's door, Narada flew straight off to the heavenly palaces of Brahma and Vishnu. "This child has effortlessly turned away Shiva; his fearsome bull, Nandi; and a battalion of the invincible Shivaganas," he told them. Narada was not one to mince words. "Watch out! What if this little boy grows stronger and stronger? He might turn you all out of Heaven! The whole world will be in turmoil! He could turn the entire universe upside down! You must act now!" Of course, when they heard this, Brahma and Vishnu could not simply sit and wait. They decided to consult with Shiva, and Shiva was happy to accept their help.

Because children in India are taught to respect their elders and politely do whatever they ask, the three gods decided that Brahma should disguise himself as an old professor with a long beard and scholarly robes. He would go to the door where the boy stood guard and try to reason with him. Surely the child would step aside for a kind old teacher.

"My dear young man," said Brahma, "you must put that wand down and let me through at once. Don't be silly, now. I can see you are a well-behaved, smart little boy. Surely you know enough to obey your elders. There is no reason to stand here driving people away. No one will hurt you." Brahma prattled on and on, sweet-talking and gently chiding the boy. But Parvati's son was not to be distracted from his duty. He pounced on the old professor.

"I obey only my mother! My mother told me to stand here and to let no one through." He pulled roughly on Brahma's beard. "Entry denied, sir!" he said.

When Brahma reported back to Shiva and Vishnu, Shiva decided that it was time to get tougher with the boy. "I will summon Indra, Lord of the Skies. He and his elephant vehicle move like the wind, and my own son, Kartikeya, commands Indra's army. No one can defeat him. You'll see," Shiva said with confidence. "The boy will soon be gone, sent back to wherever he came from."

So the army gathered. Kartikeya, with a huge arsenal of weapons, rode up on his impressive vehicle, a large and beautiful peacock. Indra, the king of the lesser gods, sat astride his gigantic white elephant. Indra's weapons were nothing less than the tempests themselves—thunder, lightning, rain, and hail. The air crackled with a thousand gathering storms.

On one side of Heaven, the gods nodded in approval.

But Parvati was furious. Here was a horde of ruthless soldiers, aided by the force of hurricanes, amassed against her beloved son, who faced them with only a slender wand and the strength of his courage and determination.

"This is an injustice!" she cried.

Remember that Parvati was a goddess. She could take any form she wished, and when she saw what was happening she changed herself into the fierce Nav Durga, a frightening goddess who could multiply her body over and over again. Thus transformed, she rushed to the boy's aid on the back of a fearsome tiger, shooting arrows and throwing curved daggers while the boy brandished his wand at the oncoming forces. It is Nav Durga's job to protect and defend those in need, and she has never lost a battle. With her support, the little boy won easily. The soldiers fled in terror—even the wind and thunderheads blew away.

Now the gods were really concerned. Narada's words were coming true. Never before had the gods and goddesses battled each other with such bitterness and anger. This boy was more troublesome—and more powerful—than the gods could handle. They must get rid of him!

Vishnu decided to use his ultimate weapon, the razor-sharp chakra that spun on his index finger. He summoned his eagle, Garuda, and flew to where the little boy stood guard. As Vishnu poised his finger to let loose the deadly disc, the boy hurled the full force of his wand. Spinning through the air, Vishnu's chakra sliced the wand in two.

Undaunted, the boy picked up one of the pieces and hurled it at Vishnu again.

"Entry denied, sir!" he cried.

In defense of his master, Garuda caught the wand in his powerful beak. But it had been a close call; the boy could have hurt Vishnu terribly.

Shiva, standing near, was enraged to see the boy attacking Vishnu. This boy was humiliating them all! Shiva rushed forward to help.

The boy didn't see Shiva approach. He didn't hear the trident blade slicing through the air. Shiva swung once, and with that single blow cut the little boy's head right off!

Poor Parvati watched in horror. The boy she had created and loved was dead. Her son had acted with unquestioning devotion, defying the most powerful gods to protect her privacy. He had only done as she wished. Now his body lay lifeless on the ground, his head severed dreadfully and damaged beyond repair.

A mother's grief is a most powerful force, and Parvati's anguish was equaled by an implacable anger. The sound of her cries shook the heavens, and the terrifying form of the goddess Kali sprang from her forehead. A host of other goddesses joined her, vowing to avenge the child. They rampaged like a whirlwind, laying waste to anything or anyone that stood in their way. They showed no mercy.

In desperation, Brahma and Vishnu appealed to Parvati. "You are destroying everything! Heaven will be ripped to pieces; the earth will spin off its axis. Please, we beg you, calm down."

She stared at them, eyes blazing. "You killed my son. This is *your* doing. If you want to preserve the balance between Heaven and Earth, then you must bring my son back to life."

At last the gods understood. "Parvati," said Vishnu, "we have wronged you. We will give your little boy back to you. I will search the earth and find a suitable head for him, and he will be whole once again."

And so Lord Vishnu crossed over the land, back and forth, searching for just the right creature who could donate its head to bring the boy back to life. "Too placid . . . too furry . . . too jumpy . . . too noisy . . . too scary," he muttered to himself as he passed by cows and goats, rabbits and donkeys, cats and dogs, tigers and wolves. He wanted to give the boy the strength and wisdom of the best possible animal. Finally he came upon a baby elephant, lying back to back with its mother. "Perfect!" Vishnu thought, and he woke up the baby's mother.

"Mother elephant," he told her, "there is a terrible war being waged in Heaven and on Earth. If you would spare your son, I believe we can restore order in the universe."

The mother elephant was very sad to give up her baby, but she

agreed. "When Brahma created us elephants," she said, "he gave us many valuable qualities: loyalty, strength, keen senses, long memories, calm minds, and great wisdom. I know my son will serve you well."

She stroked her baby gently with her trunk. "May you have a long and happy life," she murmured. "I will never forget you."

"Don't worry," said Vishnu. "Your son will be immortal now. No one will ever forget him." As he touched the little elephant, he passed on to the baby animal all of his love and compassion. Then he used his chakra to remove the little elephant's head, which he carried back to where the little boy's body lay.

Brahma took the head from Vishnu and placed it on the body of the little boy. As he did so, he also passed on to the child all of his own wisdom and resourcefulness. Parvati was overjoyed to see her son stretch his limbs as he slowly came back to life. She thought he looked perfect and didn't mind at all that he was different from before.

Her little boy settled happily in her lap. She put her arm around him and said, "Welcome back."

Shiva leaned forward and placed his hand on the little boy's head, blessing this new addition to the family and passing on his kindness and immense energy. "Your mother, Parvati, is my wife," he said, "so I adopt you as my son. From now on, you may call me Father."

Everyone rejoiced to see the end of the war and bloodshed. Far away, Narada watched and listened and smiled his approval.

As it happened, while Parvati and Shiva and all the other gods and goddesses were busy fighting over the boy who guarded Parvati's door, the people on Earth had been having some troubles of their own. Many of their problems were caused by Shiva's assistants, the Shivaganas, who enjoyed stirring up trouble, just for the fun of it. They loved to create confusion and arguments and delays, and lately they'd been running wild while Shiva's attention was elsewhere. The people grew more and more miserable as their problems multiplied.

There was no one in Heaven who could help them. Lord Brahma was too busy creating everything in the world. Lord Vishnu was responsible for keeping Brahma's creations healthy and prosperous. And it was Shiva's job to clear out space for new creations, so the world would not get too crowded. They had no time to help mere mortals with day-to-day questions and problems.

But now Brahma looked down from Heaven to see his creation in chaos and realized the people on Earth needed a god of their own, a friendly god who could help them with their everyday problems. They especially needed someone who could get Shiva's attention and remind him to discipline the Shivaganas when they got out of hand.

Brahma and Vishnu thought that one of Shiva's own sons would be ideal for the job. But they didn't know which son would be the better choice. It would be a job that required intelligence and resourcefulness and, most of all, wisdom.

So the gods arranged a contest between the elephant-headed boy and Shiva and Parvati's first son, Kartikeya, to see who had those qualities in greatest measure.

"This is a race," Vishnu said. He pointed to Shiva and Parvati, who sat together on a hilltop. "The starting place is at your parents' side. You need to circle the whole universe. Whoever returns first will be chosen as Shiva's representative and will lead the Shivaganas on Earth."

Kartikeya brushed his robes and showed off his weapons. Privately, he thought he and his speedy peacock would win the race. When the elephant-headed boy appeared—riding a little mouse—Kartikeya couldn't help laughing.

"You won't get far on *that*!" he said.

With much saber rattling and feather shaking, Kartikeya and the peacock soared off on their long, long journey around the universe. "I'll be back," he called, his voice fading in the distance. Then the little boy calmly hopped upon his mouse. He had chosen the unassuming mouse as his vehicle for a very good reason—the lowly mouse always manages to get anywhere it wants to go.

"Here I go," said the boy with a humble bow to everyone. He circled once around Parvati and Shiva, and then he bowed again. His mouse bowed too. "I'm back," he said.

The gods stared. "What do you think you're doing?" they asked.

"I have completed my journey," the boy explained patiently. "You, Mother and Father, are everything to me. You have given me life, just as the sun and the earth give energy to all living beings. So, I love and respect you as much as I love and respect Heaven, Sun, and Earth. When I circle around you, I circle my entire universe."

"You speak wisely," said Brahma. "You show intelligence, clarity, loyalty, and insight. We hereby give you the name Ganesh, which means leader of the Shivaganas. Your job is to help people on Earth whenever they're in trouble or in need."

To this day, the immortal elephant-headed Ganesh lives in temples, shrines, and homes all over India, helping people overcome all the obstacles that life puts before them. With love and devotion, they start each day by praying to Ganesh and seeking his blessings.

Note to Parents and Teachers

Stories from the ancient past are full of wisdom and enduring truths that continue to be relevant today. The story of Ganesh is essentially a story of a child's devotion and loyalty to his mother and of that mother's love for her child. The minute Ganesh jumps from Parvati's palm he is ready to do whatever he can to serve her, and he doesn't let anything sway him from his determined course. He bravely stands firm in the face of raging bulls, roaring hurricanes, and entire armies. It helps to have a magic wand, of course, but nevertheless, Ganesh serves as a model for modern children of someone who sticks to his principles. A child with Ganesh's strength of character wouldn't let himself be pushed around by peer pressure or the mass media once he'd set his mind on a fair cause worth defending.

Parvati, for her part, loves her child no matter what. When she feels that he has been wronged, she does everything in her power to defend him. And when Shiva commits the unforgivable act of beheading him, Parvati's grief and anger know no bounds. Because she is a goddess, her rage touches off a cosmic battle between the entire pantheon of Hindu goddesses and gods. As in all mythological stories, it is a symbolic battle, and what is at stake is the entire balance of the universe. Indian mythology gives equal value to the forces of creation and the forces of destruction—the important thing is to keep those forces in equilibrium. When he restores Ganesh to life with the head of the baby elephant, Brahma keeps the forces of destruction from spinning entirely out of control.

And Parvati, good mother that she is, loves her child as much as she ever did. His strange appearance doesn't matter to her at all. Parvati's unwavering love reminds parents that all children need unconditional love, no matter how they look or what skills and abilites they possess. By loving children fully, parents ensure the future of humanity. In today's world, where so many forces conspire to undermine the strength of the family, it is reassuring for children and parents alike to discover stories that confirm that an outpouring of energy in the form of love, loyalty, and devotion can bring families together, healing society one family at a time.

How Parvati Won
the Heart of Shiva

Harish Johari and Vatsala Sperling

Illustrated by Pieter Weltevrede

About Shiva and Parvati

The Hindu people believe that long, long ago in the ancient land of India, gods and goddesses came from Heaven to Earth to take the form of human beings whenever they wanted to. Even though they looked like humans and lived like humans, they had many amazing powers that were not at all human. They could turn into animals or trees or rocks—and then back to human form—whenever they needed to. The gods and goddesses also appeared in the dreams of people who worshipped them and gave these people special favors called boons. The people who received boons could do magical things too.

Stories from these ancient times are told and retold in India to this day. The story you are about to read is about an eternally married couple, the great mother goddess Adishakti and her heavenly husband, Shiva (Lord of All Gods). Besides being married in Heaven, whenever Shiva and Adishakti choose to take human form on Earth, they find each other and get married again. In this story Adishakti comes to Earth as the princess Parvati, while Shiva visits Earth as a wandering holy man, or yogi. Parvati knows that Shiva is the only man for her, but he's so busy meditating she can't even get him to look at her, let alone marry her.

The story actually begins with Mena, a girl who was renowned for her worship of Shiva and who later became the earthly mother of Parvati.

Mena was a young princess who was devoted to Lord Shiva with all her heart. Pleased with Mena's true devotion, Shiva had granted her a special boon—the ability to be magically transported to any place she wanted to go. Mena was happy to worship Shiva from afar, but her secret desire was to see him face-to-face someday. So when she heard that Lord Vishnu had invited all the gods and sages to his island in Heaven for a visit, she was very excited. Shiva was a dear friend of Vishnu's. Surely he would be there! All she had to do was use her special boon and go to the heavenly island herself. Her heart thumped with joy and anticipation, and off she flew.

Mena appeared first before Vishnu, whose kindness and hospitality were well known. He looked at her face, shining with love for Shiva. With a kind smile, he said, "Would you like to stay and meet my friends? Shiva will be here soon."

Mena's devotion to Shiva was so great that just the *thought* of actually seeing him put her under his spell, and she sank to the ground in a trance. As the gods and sages began to arrive for the gathering, she did not even notice their arrival. If the sages had known that Mena was under Shiva's spell, they would have understood why she didn't rise to greet them. But not knowing, they shook their old gray heads and grumbled disapprovingly. "These young folk! What disrespect!" And before Vishnu had a chance to explain, one of those wise old sages muttered under his breath, "Since you can't even get up when we come in, rude girl, one day you will end up marrying a mountain!"

When she had regained her senses, poor Mena apologized profusely and begged to be forgiven, but the curse could not be undone. She returned to Earth and roamed the land, lamenting her fate. "How can I possibly marry a mountain?" she cried. Finally, years later, she reached Himalaya, King of the Mountains. Himalaya, too, had been granted a boon from the gods that allowed him to change his form when he needed to. Most of the time he appeared as a jagged mountain range that ran from east to west, and that was how Mena found him. His mountains were the loftiest in the world, the highest peaks always capped with snow. Lower down, the foothills were covered with lush trees, and in springtime the melting snow filled rivers and ponds with fresh, cool water. Many sages lived and meditated in Himalaya's numerous caves.

Lord Shiva himself often came to Earth, taking the form of a wandering yogi. He wore nothing but animal skins, with snakes around his neck and a crescent moon in his long, unruly hair. Shiva favored the most remote places he could find and especially loved the quiet, intense cold on Mt. Kailash, the tallest of all the snow-covered peaks of Himalaya's mountain range. With Shiva as his honored guest, Himalaya was happy and content.

But when Himalaya felt the lovely Mena wandering across his spine and heard her laments, the desire for a wife grew in his heart and he hastened to appear before her in human form. Himalaya was very handsome indeed, and he was a wise soul as well. He and Mena exchanged stories, both mentioning their devotion to Shiva, and Mena began to feel that marrying a mountain might not be such a bad idea after all.

Soon Mena and Himalaya were wed. Because they both wanted children, they said a special prayer to the great mother goddess Adishakti, inviting her into their lives. Adishakti was so pleased with their prayers that she resolved to be born on Earth as their daughter. In Heaven, Adishakti was Shiva's wife. When she came of age on Earth she would find Shiva and marry him again, as always. Of course, the new parents had no idea that their future daughter would grow up to be Shiva's betrothed.

When Mena gave birth to a baby girl, she and Himalaya were overjoyed and named their child Parvati. Parvati grew to be a beautiful and independent little girl, the apple of her devoted parents' eyes.

When she was a little older, Himalaya presented Parvati with a magical flying carriage. "This will take you anywhere you'd like to go and bring you home safely," he told her. The carriage was made of gold and looked like a little floating palace. Its pillars were decorated with sweet blossoming flowers and its dome was covered with exquisite pearls. Its floor was made of transparent gemstones, and the whole fantastic contraption was powered by the sun. When Parvati traveled in her magic carriage, all eyes turned toward the sky and the mountain people waved to their beloved princess flying by.

While Parvati was still quite young, Sage Narada visited Himalaya. Narada could travel at the speed of light, reaching great distances in the blink of an eye. Very smartly, he kept the entire cosmos under his intense observation. His visits were famous because he always brought news from far-off places. He also liked to point out things that people hadn't realized before, pushing people to take action. Himalaya welcomed Narada with joy and humility—and maybe a little apprehension. He brought Parvati to meet the sage and said, "O Narada, would you please read my daughter's horoscope?"

Narada carefully watched the child and studied her horoscope. Then he cleared his throat. "Himalaya," he began, "your daughter has all the auspicious signs on her body and her horoscope is powerful. She will only bring you joy. But . . . ," he cleared his throat again, "I do see one difficulty. Her husband will be a naked yogi. He will be free from all desires and needs. He will not have any parents. His appearance and manners will be offensive and frightening."

Himalaya broke in, anxious and afraid. "What can I do to help my daughter? Is there a way out?" he asked.

Narada quickly finished explaining. "Do not worry. Parvati's bridegroom will be none other than Lord Shiva. You must make certain that she doesn't marry anyone else."

Himalaya was confused. "But Shiva sits in the wilderness in deepest meditation. He has no interest in women or marriage. How will my daughter succeed in getting his attention, let alone in winning his heart?"

"I see that you are unaware of your daughter's true identity—she is none other than Goddess Adishakti herself, Shiva's eternal wife," answered Narada. Himalaya adored his daughter all the more, now that he knew who she really was. But he kept Narada's revelation to himself.

One day, years later, Mena said to Himalaya, "It is time to find a husband for our daughter." She gazed fondly at Parvati, who had grown into a truly lovely young woman.

Himalaya turned to her gravely. "Mena, my dearest, you must teach her how to pray to Shiva. For it is he who will be her bridegroom."

Mena's eyes filled with hot tears. She knew that being devoted to Shiva was no easy task. Nobody loved Shiva more than she did, and in all these years she had never even gotten to *see* him. How could she put her daughter through such disappointment? But Himalaya told her Narada's predictions, and so she agreed to talk to their daughter. She took Parvati aside to explain gently. "You must do all you can to make Shiva happy with you. He is going to be your husband."

Meanwhile, Shiva had decided to settle on one of Himalaya's lovely mountain peaks to begin a new round of meditation. As soon as he realized that Shiva was nearby, King Himalaya brought Parvati to him. Parvati placed a gift of flowers and fruits before Shiva and stood silently. Himalaya spoke with reverence. "O Lord Shiva, I am honored by your visit. I have asked that no man, beast, or bird should trespass and disturb you. Please, let my daughter, Parvati, serve you and take care of all your needs while you are here."

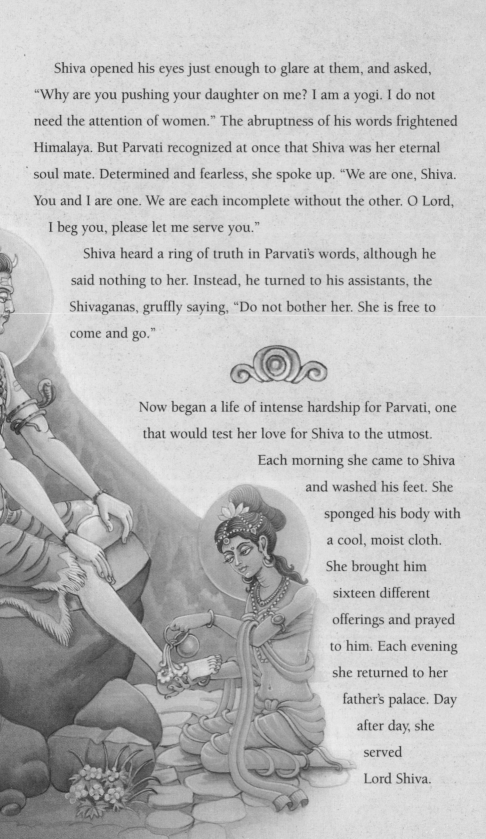

Shiva opened his eyes just enough to glare at them, and asked, "Why are you pushing your daughter on me? I am a yogi. I do not need the attention of women." The abruptness of his words frightened Himalaya. But Parvati recognized at once that Shiva was her eternal soul mate. Determined and fearless, she spoke up. "We are one, Shiva. You and I are one. We are each incomplete without the other. O Lord, I beg you, please let me serve you."

Shiva heard a ring of truth in Parvati's words, although he said nothing to her. Instead, he turned to his assistants, the Shivaganas, gruffly saying, "Do not bother her. She is free to come and go."

Now began a life of intense hardship for Parvati, one that would test her love for Shiva to the utmost.

Each morning she came to Shiva and washed his feet. She sponged his body with a cool, moist cloth. She brought him sixteen different offerings and prayed to him. Each evening she returned to her father's palace. Day after day, she served Lord Shiva.

Shiva remained deep in meditation and
took no notice of her, but Parvati's devotion
melted the hearts of all the other gods.
Indra, the king of the lesser gods, was
especially concerned for her. He
decided to ask his friends Kama and
Rati to help. When Kama and his
wife, Rati, danced, the air overflowed
with love's ardor and nature burst
joyfully into spring. And when Kama
aimed his magical flowery arrow,
whomever he hit became
filled with love's desire.

"Kama," Indra said urgently,
"please do something. Shiva must be
made to notice Parvati. Her love
cannot go in vain."

"Of course," Kama said,
jumping to his feet and grabbing
Rati's hand. "Rati and I would
do anything for Parvati's
happiness."

As Kama tiptoed around Shiva and found a hiding place from which to shoot his arrow, springtime awoke. Birds sang; their hatchlings chirped. Flowers blossomed and their sweet fragrance was carried on gentle, cool breezes. Love was everywhere—even the cruelest and most barren of hearts could not ignore the stirrings of desire.

Shiva, sensing the change in the air, suspected that Kama was somewhere nearby. But before he could investigate, Parvati, dressed in fresh garlands, appeared before him. *Oh dear, Parvati looks more beautiful than ever,* thought Shiva. Then he looked around to see Kama peeking through the bushes, aiming a floral arrow straight at his heart.

Shiva was furious that his focus and concentration had been disrupted. He turned to face Kama and with one glance he destroyed the magic of the arrow. Then the third eye in the middle of Shiva's forehead opened and a bolt of fire shot forth, consuming the unfortunate Kama in a puff of smoke. Rati let out a pitiful cry and ran desperately for help. The gods were horrified to see Kama come to such a fiery end, but there was nothing they could do. Determined to return to his meditation, Shiva vanished from the site.

Heartbroken, Parvati returned to her parents' house. They appealed to Narada for help.

"I have tried so hard!" Parvati told Narada. "What more can I possibly do to win the heart of my beloved Shiva?"

Narada answered in a soothing voice. "You must meditate on his name. Do nothing but chant *Om Namah Shivaya* and do not lose hope. For you, Parvati, nothing is impossible."

Thus began the most severe test for Parvati. To prepare herself, she discarded her jewelry and ornaments, replacing them with simple beads. She gave away her garments of soft, lustrous silk and donned rough handspun cotton. She went out to where she had last seen Shiva, her heart aching with longing. She was determined to do whatever it took to bring him back.

Parvati embraced all hardships. In the heat of summer she sat in a ring of blazing fire and chanted, "*Om Namah Shivaya.*" In the rainy season she welcomed the thunderbolts and lightning and continued chanting through the worst of the storms. In winter she let the snow bury her body up to her neck, while she kept her mind pure and focused. "*Om Namah Shivaya, Om Namah Shivaya,*" she chanted, over and over. But Shiva did not come.

ॐ नमः शिवाय ॐ नमः शिवाय ॐ नमः शिवाय ॐ नमः शिवाय ॐ नमः शिवाय ॐ नमः शिवाय ॐ नमः शिवाय ॐ नमः शिवाय

Next she spent a year eating nothing but fruits; then for another year she lived on leaves. She gave up food altogether and lived on air and water, then on air alone. Her breath could barely be heard, yet she continued chanting, "*Om Namah Shivaya.*" But Shiva did not come.

Parvati's meditation calmed the beasts around her. The ferocious animals lost their fierceness, while the weaker animals lost their fear. Tigers and lions, rabbits and deer approached quietly and sat together at her feet. The plants and trees produced plenty of fruits and leaves for all the animals and birds, and the forest became an oasis of love and peace. "*Om Namah Shivaya,*" Parvati chanted. But Shiva did not come.

वाय ॐ नमः शिवाय ॐ नमः शिवाय ॐ नमः शिवाय ॐ नमः शिवाय ॐ नमः शिवाय ॐ नमः शिवाय

Unable to bear their daughter's pain any longer, Himalaya and Mena came to Parvati. "Daughter, it's no use. Why do you continue? Shiva does not even notice you. Come back to us, dear daughter," they pleaded.

"No," Parvati said. "I will not give up. Shiva will come." She closed her eyes and continued chanting, and her parents turned sadly away.

As she focused her mind again, the melodic sound of Parvati's chanting made every cell in her body vibrate with energy. Soon sound energy became heat energy and Parvati began to glow—first like a fierce firefly, then like a brilliant lamp, and finally like a blinding fireball radiating intense waves of heat. Everything around her began to warm up until all the plants and animals and the earth itself felt scorched. And still Parvati chanted to her beloved. Even the gods began to feel that their heavenly home was becoming an inferno. They could take it no longer.

At last Brahma, Vishnu, and all the lesser gods traveled to where Shiva sat. They stood silent and humble, waiting for Shiva to end his meditation. When he finally opened his eyes, Shiva asked, "What brings you here?"

The gods joined their palms together and bowed to Shiva. "Parvati's meditation is burning up the entire universe, dear Lord. She will not give up until you recognize her love for you and marry her."

"I see," said Shiva. "I will consider . . ."

He decided to test Parvati's resolve in person. Dressed as an old Brahmin priest, he appeared before her. "What does your heart desire, my dear young yogin, that you have resorted to such a severe meditation?" he asked.

"My heart belongs to Shiva," Parvati said. "My breath is hanging on only so that I can meet him."

The old man giggled. "That silly Shiva? That ugly, homeless man has nothing to offer a girl like you. He lives in forests and burial grounds. His assistants are horrible ruffians. You'd have a life of certain suffering with him. Change your mind. Even now you have time to save yourself."

Parvati's eyes blazed with fury. "It is a terrible sin to say such things! It is an even greater sin to listen to them!"

Though she knew it was rude to turn away from one's elders, Parvati turned her back on the old Brahmin. She reached to put more wood on the fire so that she could resume her meditation. But the old man grabbed her arm and asked, "Why do you turn away from me, my dearest? You are my eternal beloved. Marry me, please."

Startled, Parvati looked up to see that the old man had vanished. Then her heart leaped, for in his place stood the love of her life, the one for whom she had endured the most difficult of trials. Shiva! At last, Shiva had come!

"Yes," she answered joyfully. "I will marry you."

To complete her happiness, Parvati wanted to tell her parents straight away. They, too, had endured hardship and sadness on her behalf. So she set off for home, anxious to let them know the good news as soon as possible.

Meanwhile, Shiva dressed himself as a street dancer and traveled separately to Himalaya's palace, singing and dancing to his own merry drumbeat. Mena treated the dancer with hospitality, and even brought him precious gifts, but he asked for only one thing—to be married to Parvati. "I am afraid that is not possible," said Mena. "My daughter has waited all her life to marry Shiva. She will not marry a street dancer like you. Please go." The dancer rejected the gifts and continued to dance. "I am here to ask Parvati's hand in marriage," he insisted.

Himalaya at length grew annoyed with the dancer and asked his soldiers to throw the man out. "Grab him!" he said. But Shiva blazed with the brilliance of a thousand suns, and no one could touch him. "Push him!" Himalaya said. But Shiva whirled in place, as solid and heavy as all the mountains put together, and no one could budge him.

Then all at once Himalaya, Mena, Parvati, and everyone else there fell under a wondrous spell. They saw Lord Vishnu with his conch, discus, mace, and lotus flower. They saw the four-faced, wise Brahma. They saw the three-eyed Shiva with his trident and moon. They saw the entire cosmos in a great swirl of bright energy all around the mysterious dancer, and their eyes were opened. Shiva himself, Lord of All Gods, was dancing joyfully in the courtyard, asking Mena and Himalaya for the hand of their daughter, Parvati.

The devoted parents held a glorious wedding for the couple and, when the festivities ended, saw them off to the blissful Mount Kailash. As Mena and Himalaya waved farewell, their eyes shone with happiness. Their beloved daughter had finally won the heart of Shiva.

Note to Parents and Teachers

Parvati and Shiva are one of the central couples of Hindu mythology. Each is the perfect complement to the other. As an aspect of the great mother goddess Adishakti, Parvati brings forth and nurtures life. Shiva, on the other hand, is often known as the god of destruction. In that ruthless aspect he must destroy life to keep the forces of the universe in balance. Western religious traditions are dualistic, viewing forces as either good or evil. The Hindu tradition takes a more holistic view. Neither creation nor destruction is seen as inherently good or bad—it is the balance between the two that is important.

The story of Parvati's efforts to win Shiva's heart is just one in a vast web of interconnected stories about the Hindu pantheon. Another story in that web provides context for this one. In that story a powerful and destructive demon named Tarakasura has tricked Brahma into giving him a boon—he can be killed only by a son of Shiva. Knowing that the childless Shiva is a wandering ascetic, Tarakasura doesn't see any sons on the horizon. So the boon renders him all but immortal, which means that the forces of destruction are in danger of spinning out of control. When Adishakti comes to Earth as Mena's daughter, Parvati, her greater purpose is to produce a son by Shiva who will be able to kill the demon and restore balance to the universe. But first she must convince Shiva to marry her.

Parvati's courtship story, taken from the *Shiva Purana*, is a story of archetypal perseverance. With the survival of the universe at stake, she knows that there is plenty riding on the success or failure of her mission. Also, as his eternal opposite, she loves Shiva with a steadfast and unshakeable devotion. Hence she has the motivation to confront all obstacles until she reaches her goal.

Parvati's story could spark an interesting discussion with children about identifying and pursuing the things that really matter to them. Parvati is in the fortunate position of possessing a clear and heartfelt goal, but, lacking such clarity, how does one figure out what would make the heart truly happy? What goal could be so important to a child that he or she would do anything to reach it? To shut out competing distractions and focus her intent, Parvati uses the Hindu device of reciting a mantra. How might today's child maintain focus toward a goal in the face of the inevitable distractions and discouragements? There are, of course, as many answers to these questions as there are children on Earth.

Ganga
The River That Flows
from Heaven to Earth

Vatsala Sperling

Illustrated by Harish Johari
and Pieter Weltevrede

71

About Ganga

The Ganga (or Ganges) is a sacred and beautiful river in India that flows from the high reaches of the Himalayas, through the northern plains, and down to the Bay of Bengal. It is named after the goddess Ganga. The story of how Ganga was born, and how she became a river, tells of a journey from places even higher than the Himalayan mountaintops—a trip from the heavens themselves. Ganga's journey is a long one, with many twists and turns, filled with tales of sorrow and joy, hardship and renewed hope.

*L*ong, long ago, the world was ruled by a powerful demon king named Bali. At first, he was disciplined and virtuous, ruling his subjects with justice and giving freely to anyone who was needy or hungry, but in time he grew as proud and arrogant as he was strong. He extended his empire to include three worlds—Earth, Heaven, and the Underworld—and even drove the gods from the heavens. He wanted to be the most powerful being in the universe.

"There are no other gods. I am the only god. Worship ME," declared Bali, and he forbade his subjects from worshipping or making offerings to any gods.

The gods, now homeless, were very unhappy. They went to Lord Brahma, the creator, asking for help. "King Bali is a menace to us all!" they cried.

The wise Brahma chided the gods gently. "You have brought this upon yourselves. I have seen you grow lazy and frivolous, while Bali has taken an oath of charity and has grown ever more virtuous and strong." The gods bowed their heads. Brahma smiled and continued. "But don't lose hope. We will go to Vishnu, and he will help you."

Vishnu Loka, Lord Vishnu's home, was set in a vast, milky sea that sustained all of Brahma's creations. The mighty five-hooded serpent, Shesha, bobbed gently on the waves. Lord Vishnu rested with his wife, the goddess Lakshmi, upon the serpent's snug coils.

When Lord Vishnu saw the entourage of unhappy gods led by Lord Brahma, he asked, "What brings you here?" The gods fell over each other in narrating their complaints about the demon Bali.

"He drove us from our homes!"

"He doesn't let anyone worship us!"

"He is invincible!"

"Help us, please," they all begged.

Lord Vishnu looked at them and said, "King Bali follows the path of virtue and cannot be defeated in battle. But I think I know just the way to trick him. Yes . . . I will go to Earth myself. Yes . . . ," Vishnu paused thoughtfully, ". . . disguised as a dwarf." He flashed a brilliant smile, with a twinkle in his eyes. "Don't worry. The heavens will soon be yours again."

Lord Vishnu loved visiting the earth. This emerald planet that Lord Brahma had created so lovingly and filled with plants, animals, and people fascinated him. In no time at all he had chosen his new earthly parents, Sage Kashyapa and his wife, Aditi. They were very wise, very old, and very poor. Pious and reverent, they prayed each day to the gods and were delighted with their angelic baby boy—who they soon realized was the holy being Lord Vishnu himself. Truly, he was the answer to their prayers! They named their new son Vamana and raised him with care and affection. Vamana never grew tall. Even when he was all grown up he remained a dwarf.

Shukracharya, a clever demon who was a royal counselor and teacher in the court of King Bali, was also quick to recognize Vishnu in the new baby boy. He knew that Vishnu had some devious reason for being born to such poor parents. He knew that somehow Vishnu would use his parents' poverty to deceive King Bali. He went straight away to warn the king.

"Beware, King Bali," he said, "Lord Vishnu is here on Earth. He is here to win back the heavens you have conquered." Shukracharya's voice was grave. "You must watch yourself. You have gone too far in your lust for power and wealth. You must stop harassing the gods," he warned.

"And one more thing . . ." Shukracharya hesitated. How could he explain? "If a small stranger comes asking for charity, you must not give him anything."

"I have taken a vow of charity," said the king sternly. "I thank you for your concern, but I cannot refuse a request for help. I cannot break my vow."

"But he will ruin you!" Shukracharya said. "He will take everything. Your kingdom, your wealth, your power!"

"I cannot break my vow," the king repeated. "As my teacher, it is your duty to help me keep my word."

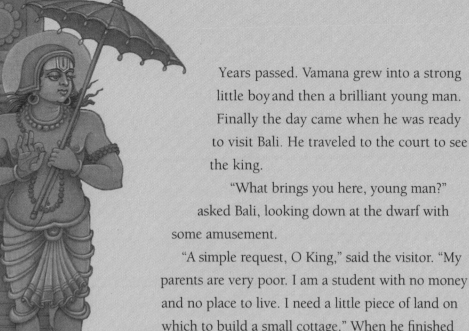

Years passed. Vamana grew into a strong little boy and then a brilliant young man. Finally the day came when he was ready to visit Bali. He traveled to the court to see the king.

"What brings you here, young man?" asked Bali, looking down at the dwarf with some amusement.

"A simple request, O King," said the visitor. "My parents are very poor. I am a student with no money and no place to live. I need a little piece of land on which to build a small cottage." When he finished speaking, a hush fell over the hall. This young dwarf seemed to glow from within. His bright eyes seemed to miss nothing.

"That is all?" asked Bali. "How much land are you asking for?"

"Only as much as I can measure in three steps," said the small stranger. With that statement, a ripple of laughter spread throughout the court. "What could you possibly measure with those short legs of yours? You'll have to build a very small cottage indeed!" the courtiers teased. The dwarf did not seem to take offense—instead, he joined in the general merriment. Soon almost everyone in the court was laughing.

But Shukracharya saw the devious smile on the dwarf's lips. He knew there must be a hidden trick, and he watched warily as the king asked for the ceremonial water jug that was used before all acts of charity. *Somehow, I must stop him!* he thought. *The king must not proceed with this gift!* Quick as a wink Shukracharya turned himself into a little fly and wedged himself tightly in the spout of the water jug. *If the king cannot pour water, the ritual cannot be completed,* he told himself with a triumphant little shake of his wings.

But the dwarf, whose eyes missed nothing, had seen the guru's transformation. "The pot seems to be stuck," he said to the king. "Allow me to clear it for you." He poked the spout with a twig. Out flew Shukracharya, buzzing frantically—the twig had poked him right in the eyes.

The king went ahead with the ceremony. He sipped from the jug three times, chanting the mantra that accompanies an act of charity, and then said, "Now, if you please, you may take three steps to measure out your land."

He turned to look down at the dwarf. But to his astonishment the dwarf now towered over him. Everyone looked up in wonder as the dwarf continued to grow, his head now lost in the clouds, now hiding the moon, his arms now encircling the sun, and now collecting the stars. He continued growing until no one was able to see the beginning or the end of him. He was everywhere. And then they heard a booming voice, calling from all around. "King Bali, in one step I have covered the entire Earth. In my second step I have measured Heaven. What shall I measure now?"

King Bali had learned his lesson. Very humbly, he bowed. "Lord, please place your third step on my head. It is all I have left to offer." The pearls in the king's golden crown shimmered, and his downcast eyes shone with tears.

Lord Vishnu recognized the true humility of King Bali's words. "Thank you," he said. "I promise I will always watch over you." Then Lord Vishnu took his third step, placing his foot on the bent head of King Bali and pressing gently. Slowly the king sank deep into the earth, down and still deeper down, all the way to the Kingdom of the Lower Realms, where he would rule forever under Lord Vishnu's everlasting protection.

The world was filled with new life. People's spirits rose as they realized they were freed from the demon's long rule, and the gods were delighted to return to their homes in Heaven.

There was new life in the heavens as well. When Lord Vishnu took his second step over Heaven, Lord Brahma had taken the chance to pour water over Vishnu's big toe, catching the drops in the small jug he carried with him. One day soon after, he saw a tiny baby girl swimming and diving in the water. Lord Brahma scooped her out and placed her on his palm. "My child, do you know you have in you the divine energy of Lord Vishnu?" he whispered to her tenderly. "My precious one, I will name you Ganga and raise you as my own."

Ganga grew graceful and sweet and gave much joy to all who knew her. Her father, Lord Brahma, and all the other gods of Heaven adored her. She had a gay and lighthearted sense of humor and laughed easily—sometimes, perhaps, too easily!

Alas, one day her lighthearted laughter got her into deep trouble. When Ganga was still a little girl, Sage Durvasa came to visit Heaven. Unlike Ganga, Sage Durvasa was not known for his sense of humor. On the contrary, he was famous for his ill temper and powerful curses, and anyone who met him was very cautious not to make him angry. One day as he was out walking, he bumped into Pavan, the invisible god of wind. Pavan's powerful gusts caught Sage Durvasa in a small whirlwind that blew around and around him until, to Durvasa's great dismay, all his clothes began to blow right off him! He clutched at his shawl, but every time he wrapped it around him the wind would tug it right off again. Try as he might, the surly sage could not gather his clothes together. After all, who can catch the wind? The gods knew enough to turn their faces away. Even if they were amused, they had the sense not to show it. But little Ganga had no sense. She pointed and laughed gaily.

Sage Durvasa could not stand to be made fun of. Grimly hanging on to his clothes, he wheeled around in terrible anger. "Girl, you need to learn proper manners. You are a disgrace to Heaven. You mock the saints! You have no place here! You must leave! You must go to Earth as a river," the sage cursed. "When humans wash their dirty clothes in your water, you will realize what a privilege it was to live in Heaven!"

Ganga cried, "Please pardon me. O Sage, I am sorry that I laughed at you. Please, please release me from your curse. I won't misbehave again! I don't want to be a river!"

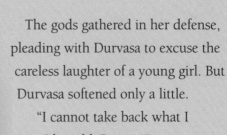

The gods gathered in her defense, pleading with Durvasa to excuse the careless laughter of a young girl. But Durvasa softened only a little.

"I cannot take back what I give," he told Ganga. "I gave you a curse—a well-deserved curse—and you must go to Earth when you are called. But I see that you are sincerely sorry. I will give you a blessing too. As a river, you will be worshipped as long as you live on Earth. Your water will purify the souls of men and release them from their sins."

Ganga was heartbroken at the thought of leaving her home and friends. All the other gods were also shocked and saddened that they would eventually have to lose their darling Ganga. But Ganga had a good heart, and after thinking it over, she realized that she had been given the chance to help ease human sorrows. In turn, this thought eased her own burden of sorrow and even gave her hope as she waited for the moment she would be called to Earth.

That moment was still some years away. On Earth, battles were being won and lost, kingdoms rose and fell, leaders came to power and then were defeated. Of all the leaders, King Sagar was one of the most ambitious. It was his goal to rule the entire planet.

In those times, there was an established custom to avoid unnecessary war. When a king decided to invade a neighboring land, he could send a single powerful horse, accompanied by an army, rather than simply launching a bloody attack. It was understood that people in the neighboring territory could either choose to capture the horse, thus inviting battle, or let the horse alone, thus signaling that they surrendered. So King Sagar sent a powerful steed, decorated with great finery and expensive ornaments, throughout all the territories and countries of the earth. Because the king's power was well known and respected, his horse was never captured. Leaders and citizens from every corner of the earth accepted his rule. When he had conquered Earth, the ambitious king sent the mighty horse galloping toward Heaven.

Needless to say, the king of the gods, Lord Indra, was not at all pleased. He had no desire to be ruled by King Sagar. Lord Indra caught the horse and led it to a desolate marshland. No one was in sight except a holy man, Sage Kapil, who was deep in meditation and did not notice when Lord Indra tied the horse to a tree nearby.

King Sagar's army, made up of his sixty thousand sons, searched high and low, looking for the horse. When they found it near Sage Kapil, they accused the sage of stealing it. "You're a thief! You're only pretending to meditate!" they shouted angrily.

Needless to say, the sage was not at all pleased either. No one likes to be accused wrongly, and he was furious to be so rudely interrupted. When he saw the clamoring army, he shot a ray of white-hot fire at them from his eyes. In a single flash all sixty thousand were burned down to a small pile of ashes.

Meanwhile, King Sagar grew more and more worried as weeks, then months, then entire seasons passed with no news from his army. Finally he sent out his only remaining son, Anshuman, to investigate.

When Anshuman reached the hermitage of Sage Kapil, he learned the terrible news. The horse was still there, grazing under the tree, but all that remained of his sixty thousand brothers was a heap of smoldering ash. "Your brothers have been consumed by my yoga fire, and their spirits are trapped," said the sage. "Only the holiest of water can purify them. You must ask Lord Brahma to send Ganga to Earth. She was born of water that touched the holy feet of Vishnu. Only she can wash the ash and release the souls of your brothers." Sage Kapil handed Anshuman the reins of the horse. "Your horse is safe. Take him and go back to your father."

Anshuman thanked the sage respectfully and returned with a heavy heart to his father. The king was overcome with grief to hear the fate of his many sons. He gave his crown to Anshuman and went into the forest alone to pray. "Oh Brahma, please release the souls of my sons!" But there was no answer from the gods, and within a short time the old king died of a broken heart.

When
Anshuman
became old, he,
too, handed over the
throne to his son and went into
the woods to pray to Lord Brahma. And he, too, failed to get a response
from Heaven. Like his father before him, he died a sad old man. His son
followed in his footsteps, and his son's son after him, and so on through
many generations, each king dying in lonely and unanswered prayer in
the forest.

Then finally, in the seventh generation, Prince Bhagirath broke the
hopeless cycle. Unlike the kings before him, Bhagirath did not wait to
grow old before dedicating himself to a life of prayer. Instead, he gave
up his power and wealth when he was a young man and went into the
forest to live a life of purity and prayer. He sat beneath a tree, meditating

piously, and in time he came to resemble the figure of a holy man, with a long beard and a glowing aura. And unlike the kings before him, Bhagirath found that his prayers were answered.

Pleased with the young prince's sacrifice and determination, Lord Brahma appeared to him and asked, "What do you desire, son?"

"Lord Brahma, I beg of you to send your daughter Ganga to Earth. The spirits of my ancestors are trapped in a mound of smoldering ash. Only Ganga can set them free." Bhagirath spoke with great humility and reverence, which impressed Brahma.

"I will ask Ganga to go to Earth," Lord Brahma replied. "But if I let her go wild, her power would be uncontrollable. She would overwhelm the earth with flooding and destruction. First you must pray to Lord Shiva to restrain her," Lord Brahma said, and then he disappeared into the sky above.

Bhagirath
began another
long and difficult
time of prayer.
Standing balanced on the
tiptoes of his left foot, his right
leg bent and his hands together, he
closed his eyes and repeated the mantra
to call Shiva. He became so completely
absorbed in his prayer that he didn't even
realize when Shiva arrived.

"Open your eyes," Lord Shiva said to him
in a rumbling voice. "You have done well. I will
be happy to help you."

As Bhagirath watched in awe, Shiva let
his hair loose. He shook his head once and
his matted locks spread out and covered
the entire earth like a veil of dark and
shimmering silk. "Ask Ganga to come
now," he said.

Ganga, taking the form of a river,
cascaded down from the heavens in
a wild torrent. A swirling stream of
shining water connected Heaven
to Earth—but only for an
instant. Then Ganga fell into
the net of hair Lord Shiva
had cast for her. With
one fluid motion, Shiva
gathered his hair in a
giant knot on the top
of his head, trapping
the river Ganga within.

Then Shiva sat down right where he was and resumed the meditation he had interrupted to answer Bhagirath's prayer. He stared straight ahead and didn't pay any attention to Ganga, who waved her arms and screamed, "Set me free! Set me free!" Shiva didn't pay any more attention to Bhagirath either. Bhagirath was confused and upset. He knew that it would be impolite to bother Lord Shiva when he was meditating. But how could Ganga help his ancestors when she was trapped in Shiva's hair? Finally, in desperation, he blurted, "Lord Shiva, we need Ganga on Earth. Please, have mercy on my poor ancestors. Please, Lord Shiva, let her loose!"

Once more, Lord Shiva heard him. He squeezed one of his locks and Ganga came rushing out again, but not as wildly. "Follow the prince," Shiva said, and he vanished into thin air. Bhagirath was elated, and Ganga bubbled with pleasure to be free, as she dropped from the icy peaks and valleys of the Himalayas. Down and down she flowed, following Bhagirath, who walked ahead blowing a conch shell. As the melting snows from the mountains joined her, she grew ever deeper and wider.

By the time they reached the plains of northern India, Ganga was a huge river, though she herself did not yet recognize how great she had become. One day as she followed Bhagirath past a holy hermitage, she heard the chants of Sage Janu and his students. She stopped briefly to listen to the lovely singing and did not notice that her banks overflowed as if stopped by a dam. She did not realize what havoc she was creating. Monks and students fled the rapidly rising water, and the sacred pots used in worship floated away. The river continued to rise, flooding temples and houses.

Sage Janu, a wise man indeed, understood just what was happening. *Ganga has come from Heaven,* he thought. *She doesn't know her own powers. There is only one thing to do.* He quickly chanted a mantra and then took a long sip of the raging waters. The flood subsided. The river vanished. All that remained were the drenched students, the sacred pots scattered about the courtyard, and a dry riverbed.

Bhagirath, walking ahead, turned his head at the sudden silence. Where was Ganga? Where was the mighty river? He ran back to the hermitage. "Ganga, Ganga, where are you?" he called frantically.

Sage Janu was sitting peacefully under a tree. "Here she is," he said, rubbing his enormous belly. "She has no self-control," he said with a satisfied burp. "She needed to learn some respect."

Bhagirath flung himself on the ground. "Please release her," he said. "I have struggled so hard to bring her to Earth!" In desperation he narrated the long, sad story of his sixty thousand ancestors, how they died, and how they were cursed, their spirits trapped in their own ashes. He told the sage of his years of solitary prayer and penance, of his meetings with Brahma and Shiva. "Please, let her go. Earth needs her now."

The sage was moved by the tale and by Bhagirath's deep sincerity. "I will help you, of course," he said. "Here she is," he said, and right away he gouged a deep cut in his thigh. Bhagirath stared in wonder. Instead of blood, Ganga poured from the wound, clear and pure. She had calmed her exuberance and was wiser from the experience of being swallowed up. Happily, the two thanked the sage, who blessed them as they set off again on their journey.

Everywhere they went, the earth responded with new life. Everything Ganga touched was renewed by her goodness: flowers opened in a rainbow of blossoms, crops grew lush and green, and throngs of people came to bathe, chanting praises, offering prayers for their ancestors, their spirits renewed and purified by her pure waters.

Ganga and Bhagirath traveled all the way across India and reached the desolate marshlands at the far eastern shores of India, where they found Sage Kapil. The old man was delighted to see them. "I have waited many, many years for this day," he said. He led Ganga to the heap of ashes—all that remained of the army. As Ganga poured her waters through the ashes, the spirits of the sixty thousand brothers emerged, lit up with divine light. Bhagirath was filled to the brim with joy. At last, the souls of his ancestors were free! The spirit beings rose like a luminous cloud, offering prayers to Ganga and showering Bhagirath with flowers as they ascended to the heavens above. And Ganga, too, was filled with joy. She had found her purpose on Earth. She was truly needed.

From that day, humans have continued to come to Ganga for help. Her sacred waters are believed to contain the energy of Lords Brahma, Vishnu, and Shiva and to have the power to release the human spirit from pain and despair. Thousands of hermitages, temples, shrines, and sacred sites have sprung up along her banks over the many thousands of years since her journey first began. Millions of people worship her, traveling great distances to bathe in her water, bringing her their woes, seeking her comfort.

So Ganga, the river goddess who made the long journey from Heaven to Earth, is still a wondrous and mighty river, flowing from the highest peaks of the Himalayas down to the Bay of Bengal. She continues to make the long journey every day. And because she touches the lives of all who come to worship her, listening to their troubles, easing their pain, and washing away their sins, her journey is still filled with tales of sorrow and joy, hardship and renewed hope.

A Note to Parents and Teachers

This story, peopled by gods, kings, and demons, is actually about the values that empower regular human beings. Though he is a demon, King Bali is highly disciplined and generous to his own subjects. His virtues have earned him enough power to kick the less-disciplined gods out of Heaven, but too much power weakens Bali's character.

He falls when he allows mockery to cloud his judgment. When Lord Vishnu approaches his court in the guise of Vamana, the whole court mocks him, leading Bali to discount his teacher's warnings and underestimate the dwarf. As a result, he loses his entire kingdom. Mockery costs little Ganga her joyful life in Heaven too. She earns the curse of becoming a river on Earth by mocking Sage Durvasa. And the sixty thousand sons of King Sagar are turned into a heap of ash for mocking an innocent man—Sage Kapil.

In contrast, Prince Bhagirath's humility and determination help him succeed in his mission to bring Ganga out of Heaven to release the souls of his ancestors.

He is remembered to this day as a humble man whose strength of character and perseverance earned their just reward.

Ram the Demon Slayer

Vatsala Sperling

Illustrated by Pieter Weltevrede

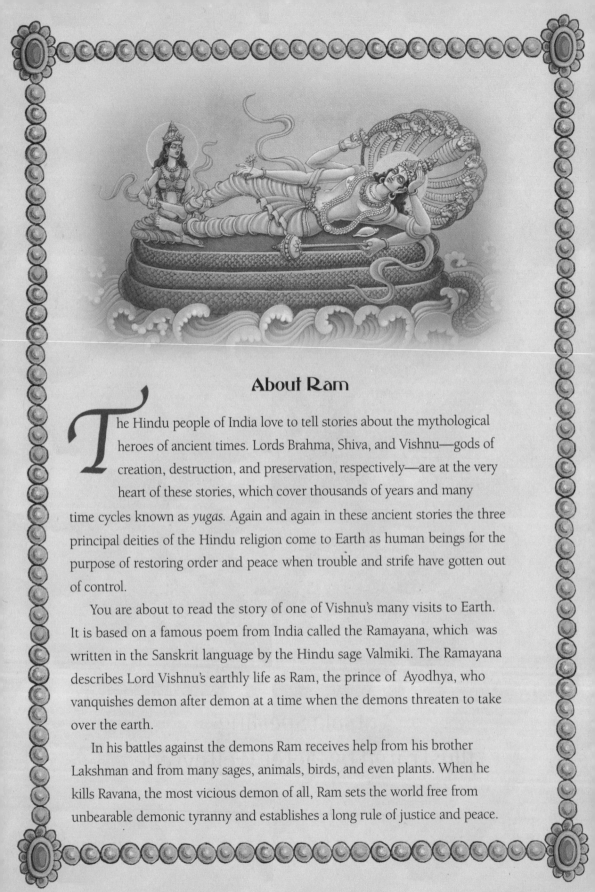

About Ram

The Hindu people of India love to tell stories about the mythological heroes of ancient times. Lords Brahma, Shiva, and Vishnu—gods of creation, destruction, and preservation, respectively—are at the very heart of these stories, which cover thousands of years and many time cycles known as *yugas*. Again and again in these ancient stories the three principal deities of the Hindu religion come to Earth as human beings for the purpose of restoring order and peace when trouble and strife have gotten out of control.

You are about to read the story of one of Vishnu's many visits to Earth. It is based on a famous poem from India called the Ramayana, which was written in the Sanskrit language by the Hindu sage Valmiki. The Ramayana describes Lord Vishnu's earthly life as Ram, the prince of Ayodhya, who vanquishes demon after demon at a time when the demons threaten to take over the earth.

In his battles against the demons Ram receives help from his brother Lakshman and from many sages, animals, birds, and even plants. When he kills Ravana, the most vicious demon of all, Ram sets the world free from unbearable demonic tyranny and establishes a long rule of justice and peace.

At the southern tip of India, among the tall and mighty waves of the Indian Ocean, lay nestled the small island country of Lanka. This beautiful island was blessed with azure skies, green forests, and golden beaches. But Lanka's ruler was Ravana, a terrible demon with ten hideous heads and a mean and greedy spirit. Whenever he wanted, he could sprout twenty arms as well. He also happened to be the grandson of the mighty god of creation, Lord Brahma.

Not content with his many powers, Ravana prayed to Brahma, insisting, "Make me immortal! Let no god or demon, animal or plant harm me!"

Brahma raised his eyebrows and asked, "What about humans?"

Ravana raised a dozen fists and sneered. "They have only two little arms, Grandfather. I have no fear of them."

So Brahma did as Ravana requested. And things on Earth went from bad to worse as Ravana and his fellow demons went on one rampage after another. Desperate cries for help could be heard from all corners of the earth. Finally Brahma had had enough. He called on his fellow deity, Lord Vishnu, God of Preservation. Pointing down at Lanka, he said, "Since I granted Ravana eternal protection, there's nothing I can do to stop his cruelty. But, he was arrogant enough to think he would be safe from all men. If you go in human form, you will be able to destroy him once and for all."

Vishnu readily agreed. He had already been born on Earth many
times to fight other demons and quite enjoyed life as a human.
Of course, his wife, Goddess Lakshmi, would be born on Earth too.
No matter where Lord Vishnu incarnated on Earth, Lakshmi always
found him and they always got married to each other.

Soon enough, Vishnu picked out his new earthly family. The kingdom
of Ayodhya was ruled by a wise and just king, Dasharatha, whose
one deep regret had always been that he had no children.
Following the advice of a holy sage, the king
performed a sacred fire ceremony, praying to the
gods with all his heart for children. And there, in the
midst of the flames, a divine being appeared, offering
Dasharatha a golden bowl filled with sweet rice
pudding.

"Take this gift from the gods and give it to
your wives," the being said, "and your childless
days will be over."

The three queens ate every bite, and before
long all of them became mothers. Kausalya, the
gentle and pious first queen, gave birth to Ram,
the incarnation of Lord Vishnu. Kaikeyi, the
valiant second queen, had once saved the
king's life in battle. She named her
baby Bharat. He was the incarnation
of Lord Vishnu's conch shell and
represented the clear voice
of truth. The youngest queen,
Sumitra, gave birth to twins,
Lakshman and Shatrughn. Lakshman
was the incarnation of Lord Vishnu's
serpent, the fierce and faithful Shesha,
while Shatrughn was the incarnation
of Lord Vishnu's powerful mace.

With four babies to care for now, the new parents were happily occupied. Soon the babies grew into lively, high-spirited little boys, and then into handsome, intelligent young men. The royal counselor, Sage Vasistha, was responsible for their education, and under his tutelage they learned how to govern like kings, ready to take any challenge. And this was a very good thing, for soon enough their skills would be put to the test.

One afternoon there came a desperate pounding at the palace door.
It was Sage Viswamitra. "We need help! Our forests are overrun with
terrible demons!" he cried. "Send Ram with me. He can get rid of them."

Dasharatha was reluctant to let his sons go, but Ram accepted the
challenge calmly, and he and Lakshman followed Sage Viswamitra into
the dense and dangerous wood. As they walked, the path grew darker,
and the air grew cold and silent. Ram listened for signs of life, but there
were none. "O Sage, what has happened here?" he asked gravely.

"You are in the land of the demon Tataka. She has stripped the
forest of all living things. The rivers and streams have dried up. Now
she eats anyone who passes by." Then the sage drew a quick, harsh
breath. "Watch out," he hissed in warning. "Here she comes."

They turned to see a huge, misshapen demon, her crooked fingers
reaching toward them, her dreadful snout hungrily sniffing the air.
Quickly, Ram let fly an arrow straight at her heart. With a long howl,
she fell across the path. A sigh of relief rose from the floor of the parched
forest as the demon died. In the distance, a bird began to sing.

"Well done," said the sage, breathing his own sigh of relief. "But
beware," he continued. "There are other demons who use trickery and
deceit. You will need sacred weapons."

They found a quiet spot at the bank of a river. As the sage began reciting secret mantras, the sacred weapons appeared. Ram sat motionless. Gleaming swords and burnished shields, glistening arrows and spears, one by one, merged into his body. He was aglow with divine power.

Suddenly, the sky turned ominously dark. The air filled with the sound of roaring thunder. This was no storm, however. It was two demons, Maricha and Subahu. This monstrous pair was in the habit of bothering humans with all sorts of mischief. One of their favorite tricks was to grind up the remains of dead animals and pour the horrid stuff all over people when they gathered to pray to the gods.

"I'll take care of them," said Lakshman grimly, fitting a deadly arrow to his bow. But Ram put out his hand to stop him.

"No, Lakshman," he said. "These demons are only causing mischief. The punishment must fit the crime." Ram let loose his own magic arrow, which snagged the two meddlesome creatures and carried them up through the air, over the mountaintops, right to the middle of the ocean. There it let them go, and— splash—they fell into the water, spluttering in surprise but unhurt.

"Well done," said the sage again.

On their way back to Ayodhya, Sage Viswamitra said they would stop at the palace of King Janak, ruler of Mithila. The sage told them Janak's story as they walked along the winding trail through the forest. King Janak, like Dasharatha, had longed for a child for many years. One day, around the same time that Ram and his brothers were born, the king found a golden pitcher buried in his garden. Lying inside was a beautiful baby girl. With heartfelt thanks to Mother Earth, he named the baby Sita and raised her as his own. Several years later, Lord Shiva paid Janak a visit and gave the king his own bow and arrow. He told Janak to keep it safe until Sita was old enough to marry. "Let each suitor try his hand. Only Lord Vishnu can lift up this bow and break it in two. Vishnu, and no other, will marry your daughter."

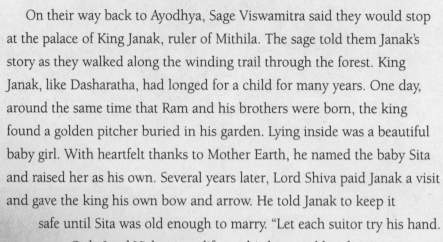

When Sage Viswamitra and the princes entered King Janak's court, they found him slumped over in despair. "Will my daughter ever find a husband?" the king groaned as a host of suitors staggered about, complaining and moaning about their unsuccessful attempts to lift the bow. Viswamitra asked Ram to try.

Ram approached and bowed humbly, first to the king, then to the sage, and finally to the sacred weapon. Then, with one easy and fluid motion, he picked up the bow, fitted an arrow, and pulled the string. The arrow sped to the sky, and with a resounding *crack* the bow snapped into two pieces. The other suitors gaped in surprise. King Janak was delighted and relieved. His daughter, Sita, blushed quietly with happiness as Ram smiled in her direction.

"Very well done," said the sage, clapping his hands.

Amid pomp and gaiety, Sita and Ram were married. They made a splendid couple. After all, theirs was a match made in heaven.

"Ram is ready to be king now,"
King Dasharatha said to Sage
Vasistha. "I am growing old, and it
is time for me to rest."

The news of Ram's forthcoming
coronation spread quickly through the
kingdom of Ayodhya. All the citizens
danced in the street. All but one, that is. Queen
Kaikeyi's maid, Manthara, was a malicious and
unpleasant old woman who collected grudges like other
people collect trinkets. She never forgave anyone for anything.
When Ram was just a little boy, he had flung a mud pie at her by mistake.
How the memory still stung! She had vowed to put him in his place one
day. And his place, she decided, would definitely not be the throne!
So, that evening, as she brushed Queen Kaikeyi's hair, she said, "I hear
Ram has been chosen as the next king. You must be very disappointed,
for Bharat's sake."

"Why do you say that? Ram will be a great king," said Kaikeyi.
"Besides, Bharat is second son."

The two women's eyes met in the mirror. Kaikeyi sighed and said,
"The son of the first queen inherits the throne. Nothing can change
the law."

"My most honorable queen," Manthara said slyly, "do you not
remember how you saved the king's life on the battlefield so long ago?
Do you not remember his promise to you?"

"What are you trying to say?" asked the queen.

"He will grant you anything. Two wishes . . ." whispered Manthara. "Do this for Bharat! Ask the king to banish Ram from the land for fourteen years and give the throne to Bharat." Manthara's eyes glittered with malice.

"Leave me alone, Manthara!" Kaikeyi cried in confusion. The old maid set down the brush and crept from the room. Then she rubbed her gnarled hands together with evil glee.

When King Dasharatha knocked at Queen Kaikeyi's door he found her distraught, sprawled on the floor with her long black hair in tangles. "What's the matter, my brave young queen?" the king asked gently. "What can I do to help?"

"You once promised you would give me anything," the queen said in a low voice.

"Of course I remember, dearest. I owe you my life," the king said soothingly.

"Then banish Ram from the land for fourteen years," Kaikeyi said, "and make Bharat the next king." There was a long ominous silence.

Finally the king spoke. "You cannot be asking this."

"Yes, I can," said the queen.

The king's voice cracked with sorrow. "Then I must keep my promise."

In the morning, the king sent for Ram. But his grief was too great, and he was unable to speak. Finally Kaikeyi explained the king's promise. Ram took in the situation calmly, but Lakshman was furious with this news.

"Lakshman, do not speak ill of our mother, Kaikeyi. And dearest Father," he said gently, turning to the king. "I am relieved it is nothing more serious. I will gladly honor your promise to Kaikeyi. Please, do not worry."

But the poor king was inconsolable. "Son," he cried, "fourteen years is too long a time. I am an old man. I am afraid I will never see you again."

It was a terrible time for the kingdom. Ram left on his long journey, accompanied by Sita and Lakshman. And soon after, the good King Dasharatha died of a broken heart. Bharat, who had been visiting his grandfather, returned to a cloud of gloom. When he learned what had happened, he confronted his mother, his clear voice ringing with the truth. "You were wrong to ask this of our father. I do not want to be king. I will find Ram in the forest and ask him to return to his rightful place on the throne."

But when Bharat found Ram in the wilderness, Ram would not agree to return. He had promised to honor his father's word, and no amount of cajoling could persuade him to change his mind. So in the end Bharat brought Ram's sandals home and placed them on the royal throne. For the next fourteen years he ruled Ayodhya as Ram's representative.

Meanwhile, Ram, Lakshman, and Sita sought haven in the dense Panchavati forest near the Godavari River. They chose a small clearing in the woods, and Lakshman built a cottage. "We will be safe here," he said, looking around with satisfaction.

But no one is ever safe from the demons. The first to find them was the demon Shurpanakha, Ravana's younger sister. She arrived in the form of a slender young maiden, smiling flirtatiously and looking from one to another. "Marry me, handsome prince," she said to Ram, "I am all yours." But Ram and Lakshman saw through her guise at once. Lakshman shot her with an arrow, chopping off her nose. She changed quickly into her true demon form. "You will pay for this, Lakshman!" Shurpanakha cried.

Next came the army of Khara and Dushana, Shurpanakha's older brothers. But Ram was ready, showering the advancing demons with divine deadly fire. Shurpanakha witnessed this disaster and rushed off to see Ravana. She told him everything that had happened. "You must avenge the insult to me! Avenge the death of our brothers! Kill the mortals! Take the beautiful maiden as your prize!" she yelled angrily.

At the mention of the beautiful maiden, Ravana sat up. "The men will die," he declared, waving several arms in the air. A greedy smile spread over each of his faces. "And the girl will be mine!"

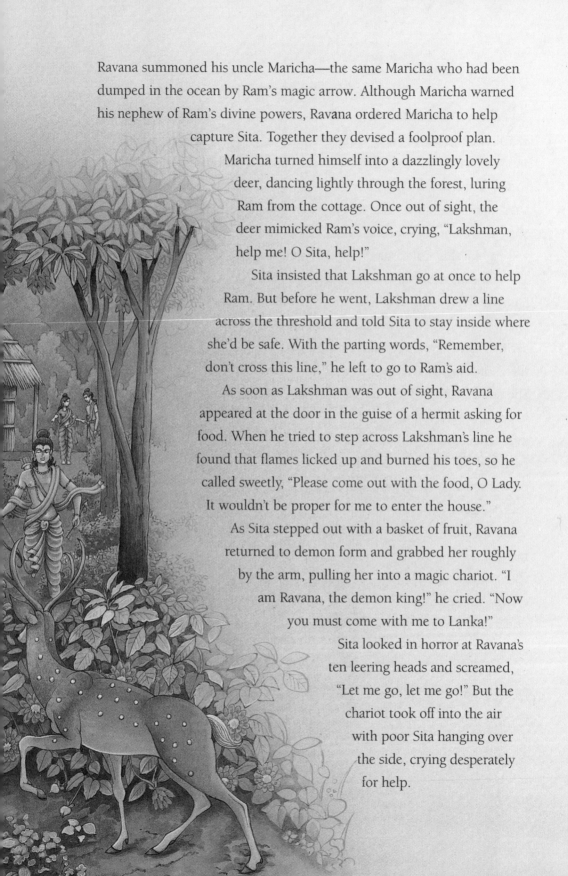

Ravana summoned his uncle Maricha—the same Maricha who had been dumped in the ocean by Ram's magic arrow. Although Maricha warned his nephew of Ram's divine powers, Ravana ordered Maricha to help capture Sita. Together they devised a foolproof plan.

Maricha turned himself into a dazzlingly lovely deer, dancing lightly through the forest, luring Ram from the cottage. Once out of sight, the deer mimicked Ram's voice, crying, "Lakshman, help me! O Sita, help!"

Sita insisted that Lakshman go at once to help Ram. But before he went, Lakshman drew a line across the threshold and told Sita to stay inside where she'd be safe. With the parting words, "Remember, don't cross this line," he left to go to Ram's aid.

As soon as Lakshman was out of sight, Ravana appeared at the door in the guise of a hermit asking for food. When he tried to step across Lakshman's line he found that flames licked up and burned his toes, so he called sweetly, "Please come out with the food, O Lady. It wouldn't be proper for me to enter the house."

As Sita stepped out with a basket of fruit, Ravana returned to demon form and grabbed her roughly by the arm, pulling her into a magic chariot. "I am Ravana, the demon king!" he cried. "Now you must come with me to Lanka!"

Sita looked in horror at Ravana's ten leering heads and screamed, "Let me go, let me go!" But the chariot took off into the air with poor Sita hanging over the side, crying desperately for help.

Jatayu, King of the Vultures, soaring above on the warm winds, heard
Sita's pitiful cries. He swooped down to rescue her, but Ravana pulled his
sword and chopped off the brave bird's wings. This brought fresh tears
to Sita's eyes. But then she spied a few monkeys sitting on a
hilltop. She took off her jewelry, tied it into a bundle,
and threw it down. The monkeys
looked up to see the chariot
and heard her calling
Ram's name.

Meanwhile, back at the cottage, Ram and Lakshman had returned to find Sita gone. There were signs of a struggle. Squashed and broken fruits were scattered over the ground. Ram turned to Lakshman, his face drained of color. "What has become of my beloved Sita?" he cried.

The brothers set off immediately and soon came upon Jatayu, lying mortally wounded in the bushes. "Ravana has taken Sita to Lanka. Hurry! I tried my best, but . . . I'm so sorry," gasped Jatayu, and breathed his last.

Ram and Lakshman gave the valiant vulture king a decent burial, then hastened farther south. They were encouraged when they met the monkey Hanuman, son of the wind god, who took them to meet the king of the monkeys, Sugriva. They found Sita's bag of jewels there, with the monkey king.

Sugriva lived in exile after losing his kingdom and his wife to his wicked older brother. So Ram and Sugriva promised to help each other. Ram would go after Sugriva's brother and Sugriva would send search parties in every direction to look for Sita.

"You go to Lanka," Ram said to Hanuman. He gave Hanuman his royal ring, saying, "Take this. You might need it."

Hanuman had a special boon that enabled him to fly through the sky at the speed of lightning and to change his size and form as he pleased. He jumped over the ocean, reaching the beautiful island of Lanka in the blink of an eye. But as he swung through the trees of the forest, he came upon something very unsightly indeed. A ten-headed demon crashed through the underbrush, an entourage of grisly monsters behind him. This ugly creature stopped under the very tree where Hanuman was perched and began to speak in a loud, unpleasant voice. Hanuman peered through the leaves and saw a beautiful young woman sitting at the base of the trunk.

"Marry me! Marry me!" the demon shouted. The woman answered angrily. "You come here day after day and make the same ridiculous demand. I will never marry you. One day my husband, Ram, will kill you on the battlefield."

Grumbling, the demon slouched away. Hanuman jumped down from the tree. "Salutations, Sita. I am Ram's servant, Hanuman." He showed her Ram's signet ring.

Sita's face cleared. She smiled but said urgently, "Tell my husband to hurry! Only he can set me free!"

Hanuman sped back to Ram with the good news. King Sugriva and all his monkeys hooted with joy. With the help of Jambavan, king of the bears, they organized an army of monkeys and bears and began the march south. When they reached the ocean, Ram offered a prayer to the ocean god.

"My monkeys cannot swim," he said. "Please, show us the way to Lanka." In reply, the ocean god told them to gather rocks lying on the beach and carve Ram's name on them.

"Now throw them into my waters," the ocean god instructed. The rocks bobbed like buoys on the sea, and the army of monkeys and bears stepped across lightly all the way to Lanka.

Ravana's spies brought him news of the invaders. "Ram has four battalions—one at each of our gates!" they reported.

Ravana dismissed the news with a shake of his ten ugly heads. "Those puny men and their pet monkeys cannot harm me! I am immortal!" roared the demon king.

"Your brother, Prince Vibhishana, has surrendered to Ram and joined his camp," they reported.

Ravana dismissed the news with a wave of his twenty hands. "I don't need his help. He was always sitting around praying to Vishnu. What a goody-goody! We will attack today!"

Ravana's army came on horses and elephants. The monkeys and bears fought bravely and well, but they were no match for demon magic and deception. As night came on, the demons became more sneaky; after all, they were the creatures of darkness. They would appear to fall down dead, only to pop up in another place. They mocked the monkeys and chopped them up like vegetables. But still, the battle raged on.

"We must conquer them once and for all!" shouted Ravana.

The demons tried one ruse after another. First Ravana's son Indrajeet sent a magic arrow that covered Ram and Lakshman with a blanket of poisonous snakes. But Garuda, Lord Vishnu's pet eagle, untangled the coiled mass and pulled them off the warriors. Next, Ravana awoke his other brother, the enormous demon Kumbhakarna. Kumbhakarna had a ravenous appetite. He often slept for six months at a time, but when he woke up, *watch out*—he'd be so hungry he could eat all of Ram's army for a snack—and Ravana was hoping that he would. But like their brother Vibhishana, Kumbhakarna was pious. He was devoted to Lord Shiva. He could see that Ravana was in the wrong, and he didn't want to fight Ram. Nevertheless, Ravana ordered him to go, and so, tossing a few cartloads of raw meat down his throat, he clomped into battle. Ram heard the giant's heavy footsteps in the distance and fitted his bow with Lord Shiva's special arrow. Kumbhakarna died instantly. An entire regiment of monkeys scattered as his body crashed to the ground.

Ravana raged and stormed about the palace when he heard the news. "Can no one rid me of Ram?" he cried.

"Father, I will use my Brahmastra," said Indrajeet. "Great-grandfather Brahma gave it to me. My magic arrows can decimate an entire army in no time," Indrajeet boasted as he headed for the battleground.

And Brahmastra, the most powerful of all god-given weapons, did just what Indrajeet claimed. With a shower of arrows, Brahmastra put a spell on the entire army. Ram, Lakshman, and all their soldiers fell into a deep trance, hovering at the edge of death.

Only one of the entire army remained awake. The bear king, Jambavan, was a son of Lord Brahma, so he was not affected. Also, Jambavan was a healer who knew everything about the medicinal powers of herbs. He roused Hanuman from the spell and carefully described the herbs he needed to restore life and heal wounds. "Go! Quickly, Hanuman," he said. "The herbs grow only on Sanjeevani Mountain in the foothills of the Himalayas."

Hanuman leaped over the Indian Ocean to the foothills of the Himalayas in a single swift bound. He found Sanjeevani Mountain covered with a dense forest of herbs. But it was quite dark by then, and the plants all looked the same to Hanuman. "Triangular leaves, purple flowers," he muttered to himself. "I can't tell them apart!" Finally, he began to dig at the base of the mountain. He dug until the mountain itself was loosened from the earth around it and he found that he could pick up the whole mountain and hold it in the palm of his hand.

"Aha! The entire mountain and all of its herbs wish to be of service to Ram," he said, and, taking a deep breath, he rose up into the sky. With the mountain resting on his palm, he zoomed back to Lanka.

The fragrance
of the medicinal
herbs reached the island
shores even before Hanuman
did, stirring many soldiers back
to life. Jambavan urged them to pick up the dead demons and
throw them into the ocean. Ram, whom Brahma
himself had already released from the spell, praised
the strength and faithfulness of his animal friends
and soldiers.

Jambavan then prepared amazing concoctions
from the chosen herbs and went from one soldier
to the next, offering a dose here, a poultice
there, or a few leaves to chew. Rows
of wounded and dying soldiers
awoke as if from sleep,
without so much as
a scratch left on
their bodies.

The next morning Indrajeet was back on the battlefield. He had expected to spend the day victoriously counting up the dead, but instead, Lakshman stood before him.

"Run," said Lakshman. "Run for your life."

But Indrajeet mocked him. "You can't fool me. You're just a ghost. Don't you even know you're already dead?"

In reply, Lakshman pulled out his bow. The arrow neatly sliced off Indrajeet's head and carried it all the way to Ravana. "Father, set Sita free," the severed head moaned. "Your enemies are no mere mortals. Give up, Father."

"Only after I avenge your death, my dearest son," Ravana roared—and he rushed into battle.

It was a long and bloody fight. One after another, Ram called upon the sacred weapons and aimed them at Ravana. One after another, he cut off the demon's many heads and arms. But as soon as he cut off one head, another would spring up in its place. In the blink of an eye, the demon's severed arms and legs grew back.

Ravana seemed to have an infinite capacity to heal and regenerate himself. Ram fought all day without making any progress at all. In ancient India, battles were fought only from sunrise to sunset. Ram tossed and turned all night, wondering how he could destroy this seemingly immortal being.

Help came just as the first rays of the dawn touched the sands, when the wise sage Agastya appeared before Ram. "Even the gods need divine assistance when they take human form," Agastya said. Under the early morning sky Sage Agastya taught Ram special prayers for the sun god. "Chant these mantras. Don't give up; evil is not immortal," he said. After performing his salutations to the sun, Ram headed back to the battlefield with renewed confidence. All through the day he used his heavenly weapons and called to Ravana to surrender.

But Ravana refused to surrender. "I am immortal!" he shouted, and continued to sprout new heads and limbs like so many weeds. Finally, in the long light of the afternoon, Ram knew that it was time to finish the battle. He aimed one last arrow straight into Ravana's belly button, piercing the very center of the demon's spirit.

With a look of shock and astonishment, Ravana fell. And this time, he did not get up again. The mightiest of all demons was dead, slain finally by a man who was also a god—Lord Vishnu—in human form.

Cries of "Victory to Ram the Demon Slayer" rose from every corner of the battlefield. The monkeys leaped into the air and danced. The surviving demons gladly surrendered, promising to give up their wicked ways forever.

Ram's fourteen-year exile was over at last. Good Prince Vibhishana took over the rule of Lanka from his slain demon brother Ravana, and Ram, Sita, and Lakshman returned to Ayodhya, where Ram took his rightful place on the throne. His long and prosperous rule is still remembered in India as the "golden age of Indian civilization."

Note to Parents and Teachers

The Ramayana is one of the oldest and greatest Indian epics. Though it was written thousands of years ago, its hero, Ram, is loved and respected in India to this day. What is it about Ram that has appealed to so many generations? First and foremost, it is his humility. Despite his godly origins, when he is born on Earth as a human prince Ram obeys the laws of nature and society just like anyone else. Aware of his human limitations, he courts, and gracefully accepts, help from all beings: gods and sages, plants and animals, rocks, and the water of the ocean itself.

In India, Ram is seen as the embodiment of truth and virtue— the highest of human values. He represents respect for parents and teachers, love for siblings and friends, and compassion for the weak and downtrodden. He honors spoken words and promises, which makes him trustworthy and reliable, and his bravery in the face of danger makes him stand tall among people of all ages, throughout the centuries, as the ideal hero.

Hanuman's Journey
to the
Medicine Mountain

Vatsala Sperling

Illustrated by Sandeep Johari

About Hanuman, the Magical Monkey

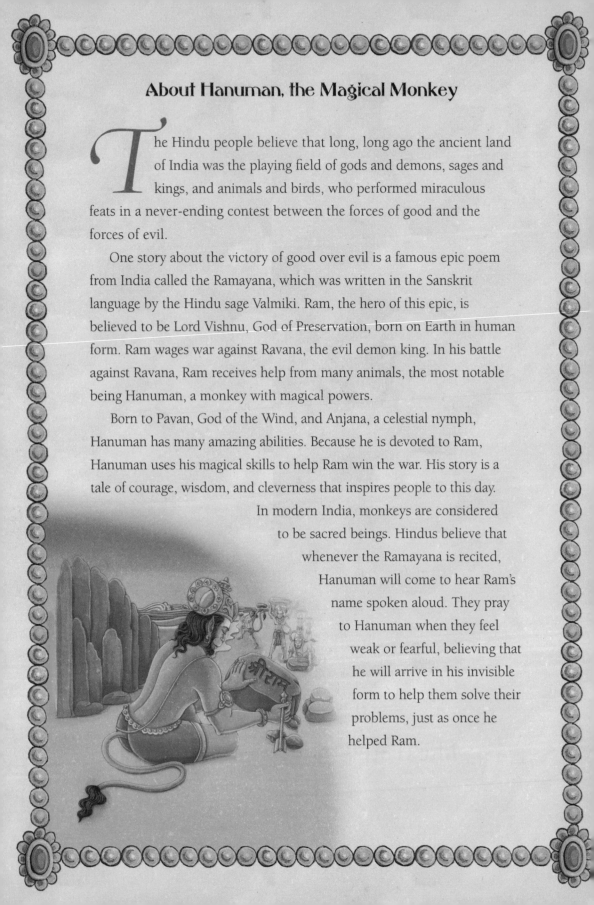

The Hindu people believe that long, long ago the ancient land of India was the playing field of gods and demons, sages and kings, and animals and birds, who performed miraculous feats in a never-ending contest between the forces of good and the forces of evil.

One story about the victory of good over evil is a famous epic poem from India called the Ramayana, which was written in the Sanskrit language by the Hindu sage Valmiki. Ram, the hero of this epic, is believed to be Lord Vishnu, God of Preservation, born on Earth in human form. Ram wages war against Ravana, the evil demon king. In his battle against Ravana, Ram receives help from many animals, the most notable being Hanuman, a monkey with magical powers.

Born to Pavan, God of the Wind, and Anjana, a celestial nymph, Hanuman has many amazing abilities. Because he is devoted to Ram, Hanuman uses his magical skills to help Ram win the war. His story is a tale of courage, wisdom, and cleverness that inspires people to this day.

In modern India, monkeys are considered to be sacred beings. Hindus believe that whenever the Ramayana is recited, Hanuman will come to hear Ram's name spoken aloud. They pray to Hanuman when they feel weak or fearful, believing that he will arrive in his invisible form to help them solve their problems, just as once he helped Ram.

It was a bright afternoon on Rishyamook Mountain and the warm sun shimmered through the leaves of the jungle canopy. Sugriva, the exiled king of monkeys, and his minister, Hanuman, were doing just what monkeys love to do—basking in the treetops, lazily grooming each other. Suddenly they were interrupted by a distant cry, the sound of a woman's voice, desperately calling, "Help, oh please help me! Ram, help me! Ram!" It seemed as if the voice was coming from the heavens, and indeed, when they looked up, they saw a flash of light, like a streaking meteor. It was a chariot, racing across the clear blue sky. As they watched, a slender arm tossed a small bundle over the side. And then, rustling in the branches, a pouch came hurtling down through the thick canopy of the forest. Hanuman, who was one of the quickest beings on Earth or in Heaven, caught it just before it hit the ground.

When the two monkeys opened the pouch, a handful of beautiful jewelry tumbled out onto the grass. "These must belong to the woman who was screaming for help," said Sugriva. They looked up at the sky again. The chariot was a mere speck, disappearing into thick clouds on the far horizon. The two monkeys looked at each other and their bright mood changed to sadness as they considered the poor woman's plight.

A few days later, a monkey scout reported to King Sugriva that he had seen two young armed men wandering near a lake. "They must be Vali's men," said Sugriva with an angry flick of his long tail. "My evil brother must have sent them to spy on me. Is he not satisfied with stealing my wife and banishing me from my own kingdom?" He clenched his fists.

But Hanuman was calmer. "We shouldn't jump to conclusions, O King," said Hanuman. "I will ask them who they are."

Hanuman, as you will see, had many amazing powers. He could change his form to whatever he liked, and he could even make himself invisible. So no one saw him as he soared above the treetops. When he reached the two men, he appeared before them as a young mendicant. Though the men were dressed in simple ocher robes, they glowed with an inner strength. Hanuman knew at once they could not be Vali's spies.

"Good sirs, with your grace and strength you look as though you could rule the world. Why do you wander in these deep and difficult woods? Please tell me who you are," said Hanuman politely.

"I am Ram. This is my younger brother, Lakshman. King Dasharatha, the late ruler of Ayodhya, was our father. My beloved wife, Sita, is missing. We are looking everywhere for her." As Ram spoke, he stared intently at the gold earring that Hanuman wore. Hanuman had worn this earring since birth, but no one had ever seen it—until now. When he was a little baby, Lord Brahma had said to him, "This earring will be invisible to all except Lord Vishnu. Born on Earth as Ram, only he will be able to see it. That is how you will recognize each other. All the magical powers I've given you will help you serve Ram."

Hanuman recalled those words and smiled. "Lord Ram, I am Hanuman." He took on his original appearance, that of a monkey, and spoke again, his eyes brimming with joy, "Climb onto my shoulders, and I will take you both to Sugriva."

On the way, Hanuman explained why King Sugriva was living in exile, and how the king's older brother, Vali, had stolen the kingdom, and had captured Sugriva's wife, Ruma. When they arrived at the top of Rishyamook Mountain, Hanuman gently lowered his passengers to the ground.

"King Sugriva, I have brought Ram and his brother Lakshman. Ram's wife, Sita, is missing, and they are searching for her," he said.

"Welcome," said Sugriva. "You are my guests and friends. We have something that might help you." Sugriva asked Hanuman to bring the jewelry pouch. When Ram opened it, he bowed his head and then held the pouch to his lips. For a moment he seemed unable to speak. Then he cried, "Sita, my beloved Sita, where are you?"

"Grieve no more, my friend," said Sugriva. "Your Sita threw this from a chariot we saw flying south. I will have the entire Earth searched for her. We will find her safe, I swear."

Ram looked up. "And in return I will help you win back your kingdom and your wife, Ruma. I know all about Vali," he said. "He shall rule no more."

Ram kept his promise right away by slaying the arrogant Vali. Sugriva and Ruma were reunited, and Lakshman held a coronation ceremony for Sugriva. The whole monkey kingdom rejoiced to have their true king back. Sugriva was very happy—so happy, in fact, that he forgot all about his promise to Ram.

Ram was patient with the lengthy celebrations, for he understood how Sugriva had suffered. But he missed Sita and grew anxious. The summer and then the rainy season came and went, and a chill settled over the land. Finally, Ram could wait no longer. Early one morning he asked Lakshman to remind Sugriva of his promise. Lakshman, who had also grown impatient with the passing months, was more than glad to help. "I'll go right now, my Lord," he said.

With a few long strides a furious Lakshman arrived at the door of King Sugriva's palace. Hanuman saw him approach and ran to alert the monkey king.

"Sugriva, it is time to get up! Quick!" Hanuman shook the sleepy king's shoulder. "Wake up! Get to your feet and keep your promise. Help Ram as he helped you," he said.

Sugriva blinked and rubbed his eyes. *Hanuman is right, as always!* he thought. He ran out the door and bumped right into Lakshman, who stood on the doorstep seething with anger. Glaring at Sugriva, he bellowed, "How dare you forget your promise to my brother?"

"Forgive me, please. I will organize a search right away," Sugriva pleaded. "Please forgive me."

"Now. Do it now," hissed Lakshman. "You must not disappoint my brother Ram."

Very relieved to be forgiven, Sugriva called for his generals and sent them off in all directions, each with a huge contingent of animal soldiers. "Look for Sita everywhere you think she could be. Look for her everywhere you think she could *never* be. Report to me in a month," he said. Then he turned to Hanuman. "You have become very close to Ram. You should ask him for your marching orders."

Ram told Hanuman to follow the path of the flying chariot. "It was headed south. You, too, should travel south to find Sita. Give her this when you see her," Ram said, and handed his gold signet ring to Hanuman. When he held the ring up, Hanuman saw the name *Ram* inscribed on it, over and over: *Ram, Ram, Ram.*

"Serving you is my honor, Lord Ram," he said with humility.

King Sugriva asked Jambavan, King of the Bears, to guide the thousands of monkey soldiers who would accompany Hanuman. Jambavan was a very wise old bear. He was the son of Lord Brahma himself and knew the answers to many of life's puzzles and deepest questions.

Marching south, the monkeys looked in all the valleys and groves, lakes and streams, cottages, townships, and kingdoms. They left no stone unturned. They asked everyone they met for information. But they found no sign of the lost Sita. And finally, they could travel no farther south. Before them was the ocean—deep, mysterious, majestic, and endless.

Their spirits fell. Monkeys, after all, do not know how to swim. "We cannot return to Lord Ram empty handed," they said. They sat in rows on the hot, shimmering sand, their pained faces bowed low. Despairing, the animals decided to fast until death.

"Did I hear you speak the name 'Ram'?" A sad old vulture appeared. Unkempt and at death's door, he interrupted the monkeys' fast with a weak croak. "I am Sampati, King of the Vultures. Jatayu, my younger brother, was killed by Ravana, King of the Demons. Jatayu tried to stop Ravana's chariot and rescue Ram's wife. He fought bravely. He tried his best, but Ravana cut his wings." Sampati's breath was ragged with grief.

"Ravana is holding Sita captive on the island of Lanka, 800 miles south of here." The poor old vulture's voice began to fade. "Now that I have told you all I know of Sita, I can die in peace." Sampati's head fell, his eyes dimmed, and his spirit soared toward Heaven.

The monkeys were happy to hear that Sita was alive, but they still had no idea how to reach her. "Maybe we can just jump to the island," suggested some of the younger, less experienced monkeys, but no one took them seriously. Monkeys can leap from branch to branch with ease, true, but they can't leap across an ocean.

Jambavan, however, knew better. "Hanuman, you never brag but I know you can cross the ocean. Let me remind you again of your birth—and all the magical boons that were bestowed upon you by Lord Brahma. Then you'll remember how you can do the impossible."

A murmur spread throughout the army. "There is hope, there is hope." Soon the murmur rose to a clamor.

"Tell us, Jambavan, tell us how Hanuman can save the day!"

Jambavan cleared his throat with a low growl and began to tell Hanuman's story.

A celestial nymph was born on Earth as Anjana, the daughter of a monkey king. When she grew up she married Kesari, the chief of another band of monkeys. She was very devoted and loyal to him. One day she took on a human form and went strolling on Rishyamook Mountain. The wind god Pavan was passing by and he saw her. She is perfect in every way, he thought. As Pavan moved toward her, Anjana felt the wind pick up, embracing her slender body, tossing her long dark hair, tugging at her silken robes. "Who dares touch me?" she asked. "I am married to Kesari. I am devoted to him."

"Anjana, it is I, God of the Wind," Pavan whispered softly. "Lord Brahma asked me to tell you that soon you will bear my son. He will be very wise and loyal to Lord Vishnu. He will be able to leap farther than the eye can see. He will be able to move even faster than I can."

"But why? Why must I bear your son?" Anjana asked.

"Lord Vishnu will need him on Earth, Anjana." Pavan whispered very softly, as quiet as thought itself.

That very evening Anjana gave birth to a little baby. He had a sweet rosy face, innocent golden eyes, and fine, sharp teeth. A sleek coat of silvery soft hair covered his agile little body. "What a perfect monkey you are, my son!" Anjana said lovingly. "Perfect in every way. Be successful in all that you are meant to do. Your father, Pavan, will be here soon to watch over you." Anjana kissed her newborn baby good-bye, and left him warm and safe at the entrance to a cave.

Baby Hanuman lay on his back, kicking his tiny feet and sucking his tiny fingers. As the night wore on, he started to feel hungry. At dawn, he noticed the rising sun.

Yum! A little plum! *he thought, and took a leap. In that one leap he*
crossed the entire sky. Higher and higher he flew.

When Indra, the king of the lesser gods, saw the little monkey open his mouth to swallow up the sun, he was horrified. "No, no, no, my child! Don't touch! Hot! Hot! Don't eat that!" he shrieked, quickly hurling a thunderbolt at the unsuspecting baby. Hanuman came tumbling down onto Rishyamook Mountain and fell right in front of the cave where Pavan was waiting for him.

Furious to see his baby treated in such a rough manner, Pavan cradled Hanuman in his arms and retreated deep into the cave—taking the wind with him. The world grew completely still. Leaves ceased their dance in the breeze, birds soaring high above on currents of air plunged to earth. All of creation held its breath.

Lord Brahma quickly approached Pavan. "You must forgive Indra. He didn't mean to harm your son. He was only trying to keep the earth from freezing to death without the sun. Come back, Pavan," he pleaded. "You are the breath of life. Both Indra and I will give your son special boons. Your little baby will never know defeat, and he will grow to be very wise, loyal, and strong. He will take after you, Pavan. He will be invisible whenever he needs to be."

Pavan was pleased, and with a strong Whoosh! he blew back into the world. The whole world took a deep breath. The trees shook their leaves with relief, and once again the birds took to the skies. Pavan agreed to let Lord Shiva and his pet bull, Nandi, take charge of raising the baby Hanuman and educating him.

Jambavan had reached the end of his story. "This is the story of your birth and all the boons that you have received, Hanuman. Sometimes, in your humility you might not remember how amazing you are. If there is one being here who can do the impossible, it is you. Now, go find Sita."

"Victory to Hanuman! Victory to Hanuman!" chanted all the monkeys as Hanuman joyfully fluffed up his fur, swished his tail, and took off over the open water with one enormous bound. They watched until he disappeared from view.

Nothing could stand in Hanuman's way. When he was gobbled up by the demon Surasa on the way to Lanka, he escaped with ease. He simply made himself as small as a fly and traveled up to Surasa's nostrils, tickling the inside of her nose. *Aachoo!* Surasa sneezed a mighty sneeze, and out flew Hanuman. He buzzed off and continued on his way before she could raise a hand to swat him.

Hanuman landed on the northern shore of Lanka just as the sun was setting. Under cover of night, he crept up to King Ravana's palace. He saw demons of all types—large and small, bony and fat. Some looked scary, some looked ferocious, some looked sneaky, and some looked mean but none of them looked sleepy. They were creatures of the night, at home in the dark.

But somewhere one of them was asleep. Of this Hanuman was sure, for he heard the faint but persistent echo of a rumbling snore. When he followed the sound to its source, he found himself facing a magnificent door, inlaid with pearls and gemstones. He opened the door gently and saw a huge golden bed, studded with thousands of diamonds. On it lay Ravana, the monstrous demon king himself. His ten awful heads rested on ten silken pillows.

Well, I've found Ravana, thought Hanuman. *But I know Sita is not here—
she would never, never stay near such a creature. I will look for her at daylight.*

The next day, Hanuman swung through the treetops, scanning the entire city for a sign of the lovely Sita. Finally he stopped in the Ashoka grove. He sat hidden among the branches of a Sansapa tree and prayed to the gods for help. As he prayed, he heard a commotion—heavy footsteps, loud snorts, and grunts grew closer and closer, louder and louder. Cautiously, he parted the thick leaves and peered out.

A huge dark form loomed menacingly, slowly approaching the very tree in which Hanuman was hiding. Many demons marched alongside the giant figure. One fanned him. Another sprinkled rose petals in his path, while another held an umbrella over his ten heads. The entire procession stopped right below Hanuman. He could almost have reached out and snatched Ravana's umbrella.

And then he looked down and saw the beautiful woman who sat beneath the tree. Sita! He had found her at last! He could barely keep himself from whooping with joy. But he quietly bided his time.

"I order you to love me, Sita," said the arrogant Ravana. "Your worthless husband can't even find me, much less defeat me in battle. Forget him. Be mine." All ten heads spoke at once, and all twenty eyes glittered with desire.

Needless to say, Sita was not the least bit charmed—nor was she afraid. "You are a fool to think I would ever love you," she said. "You came in a cowardly disguise and lured my husband away in order to steal me. You did not dare to fight Ram openly, in honest battle. Know this: I will never be yours." She spoke with indignation and contempt in her clear, soft voice.

"Beware, Sita. Do not try my patience. I will return tomorrow," Ravana said. He stomped away angrily, his entourage trailing behind him.

Sita waited until he was truly gone and then allowed herself to fall to the ground and weep. "I would rather die than be Ravana's wife! How I miss Ram! Why am I still alive?"

"So that you will be with Ram again," Hanuman whispered to her, speaking in a secret animal language in case any demons were still lurking and listening.

Sita sat up. She looked around, wiping the tears from her eyes. "Who speaks?" she asked in the same secret language.

"I am Hanuman. Lord Ram has sent me to look for you."

"How did you get here?"

"I jumped over the ocean."

"Why should I believe that? How can I be sure you are not one of Ravana's spies?"

"Will this ring prove to you that I am indeed Lord Ram's messenger?" asked Hanuman. He jumped down and showed Ram's signet ring to Sita. Sita took the ring with trembling fingers. She bowed her head and kissed it, saying softly, "Ram, my dearest, where are you? Ram, come soon and set me free." Then she gave Hanuman her barrette to take to Ram. "Thank you," she said. "What a courageous monkey you are! May your trip back be safe and swift."

But before Hanuman journeyed back, he wanted to see Ravana face-to-face. Standing there in the grove, he made himself taller than the oldest, grandest tree. Then he plucked the tree, just as if it were a rather large turnip, and swung it at a group of demon spies. He picked up huge boulders as if they were mere pebbles and hurled them too.

One of the spies ran to tell Ravana. "I saw a monkey, O King. Just a monkey. But what a powerful monkey he was! He threw a tree at my head! A HUGE tree!"

"Bring that monkey to my court! Now!" ordered Ravana.

When Hanuman saw the band of demon soldiers approaching, he shrank back to his normal size. *This is my chance to meet the demon king,* he thought to himself with satisfaction.

"Now that you have had your fun, monkey, it is our turn," the soldiers said, and they dragged Hanuman to the palace. Hanuman let them hit him and kick him. But they had no idea how powerful he really was.

"Monkey, who are you? Why are you here?" Ravana asked.

"I am Hanuman. I am here because Lord Ram sent me," said Hanuman. "Sita will never love you. Set her free, O King, and Lord Ram will forgive you." As Hanuman spoke, his tail began to grow and coil beneath him. The coil grew as tall as Ravana's mighty throne, and Hanuman, sitting atop that coil, faced Ravana eyeball-to-eyeball.

Ravana did not like hearing the bitter truth about Sita. His twenty eyes glared with rage and would not meet Hanuman's gaze.

"Kill this monkey now!" he thundered.

The demons hastened to do his bidding, but Vibhishana, Ravana's younger brother, stepped forward to stop them. "You cannot kill a messenger. You know that, Ravana. It is the law. You can injure him if you really find it necessary, but you cannot kill him."

"Burn his tail, then. That will teach him a lesson. Monkeys love their tails," ordered Ravana, glaring irritably at his brother. *Vibhishana is so meddlesome! I'll have to get rid of him soon,* he thought. He had never liked his just and truthful younger brother. Vibhishana was a great devotee of Lord Vishnu and often disagreed with Ravana's cruel policies.

The guards brought oil-soaked rags and began to wrap them around Hanuman's tail. But the tail kept growing—no matter how fast they worked, they always had more tail to wrap.

After they used up all the rags and oil from the palace, they borrowed more from the houses nearby. The tired guards wiped their sweaty brows and stretched their stiff limbs and wrapped and wrapped and wrapped. Finally, when the tail was more or less covered, they lit the very tip.

Hah! Right before their eyes, Hanuman's tail shrank back to its normal size and he bounced out the window. Soon he was hopping over the rooftops and the trees of the city. Using the tip of his tail like a torch, he started fires with every leap, until the entire city of Lanka was ablaze. Then he delicately dipped the tip of his tail in the ocean, and with a sizzle, the flame went out.

Back in the Ashoka grove, the gentle Sita saw the flames leaping above the city. She prayed, "O Fire God, please do not burn Hanuman. And please, do not allow the innocent to be hurt," and her prayers were heard.

In another long leap, Hanuman landed back on the distant shore where Jambavan, the monkey soldiers, and Ram himself awaited him. "Hurry, Lord Ram," he said. "Sita is waiting for you. She gave me her barrette to bring to you." All the animals said to Ram at once, "Lord, we'll cross the ocean with you and go to Lanka." But how could they get across?

Ram prayed to the ocean god to find a way to get the animals across the sea to Lanka. "Please help us. My soldiers cannot swim."

"You'll just need some stepping-stones," answered the ocean god. "As long as it bears your name and is thrown by Nala, the monkey general, any rock will float."

All the animals scampered around collecting rocks. Hanuman etched Ram's name on each rock and then Nala threw them all into the ocean. Before long, the string of floating rocks extended all the way to the northern shores of Lanka. The army hopped over safely, and set up camp outside the four gates leading to Ravana's kingdom.

Meanwhile, earlier that day, King Ravana had banished Prince Vibhishana from the palace. When Vibishana heard that Ram had landed, he went to join him immediately. Ram saw that the young prince was just and good, and gladly accepted him as an ally. "My evil brother has done enough harm," Vibhishana told Ram. "I will help you defeat him."

Ram gave Ravana many chances to avoid bloodshed. Time and time again, he sent the same message: "Return Sita, and you will be forgiven. Otherwise, you will pay dearly." But Ravana was too arrogant to listen. "Sita is mine, all mine!" he snarled. "Win, no matter what the cost!" he ordered his soldiers.

The demons used all kinds of trickery and dark magic but Ram's army fought valiantly and advanced on the battlefield. However, Ravana's son, Indrajeet, had the power to invoke a deadly weapon called "Brahmastra." He went to his secret grove, lit an invisible smokeless fire, whispered secret mantras to Brahma, and finally poured specially prepared hot oil on the fire from an iron ladle.

A total blackout fell upon the grove. Then out of the intense darkness arose a shimmering white chariot, pulled by four wild horses. Indrajeet mounted the Brahmastra chariot, shook the reins, and dashed to the battlefield.

"Victory to the demon king Ravana!" he shouted. The demons could see Indrajeet and his magic chariot, but he was invisible to Ram's animal army. They could not defend themselves against the fiery arrows Indrajeet rained down upon them. These magical arrows were infused with the power of the Brahmastra and spread a cloak of deep sleep over the entire army. In honor of Brahma, even Ram and Lakshman submitted to the power of Brahmastra and fell to the ground unconscious. By midday there was no one left awake to fight.

That is, almost no one. The spell of Brahmastra did not hurt Jambavan. He was, after all, Lord Brahma's son. The bear simply pulled the arrow out, rubbed his eyes, and stood up. A few steps away, Prince Vibhishana, who was also unaffected by the spell, was checking on the dead and wounded. Jambavan called to him. "Leave them for now. We first need to find Hanuman. If Hanuman is safe, everyone else will be saved too. Victory will still be within our grasp."

From across the battlefield Hanuman heard these words and sped to Jambavan. "I am fine," he said. "What can I do for you?"

Jambavan, besides being the king of the bears, was a physician as well, and he knew the healing powers of all the herbs and plants. In great haste he tried to teach Hanuman how to identify the herbs he would need, telling him what color flowers and what shape fruits to search for. "These herbs grow on Sanjeevani Mountain, the medicine mountain in the foothills of the Himalayas. Go there at once," he said. "We have no time to spare."

It took Hanuman only a few seconds to travel to the Himalayas. As he landed on the slopes of Sanjeevani Mountain he could see herbs everywhere, glowing in the light of the setting sun, their fruits and flowers sparkling like gemstones. They were beautiful and they looked powerful— but they all looked the same to him. He hesitated over one plant and then another, unsure which to pick. Finally he decided to take them all, and he began to dig at the base of the mountain. "Ah, I see the whole mountain wishes to come with me," he said with a chuckle, and he headed back to Lanka, carrying the entire mountain in the palm of his hand.

Jambavan got to work right away, preparing the concoctions and poultices from the mountain herbs that Hanuman brought to him. Under the old bear's expert care, row upon row of unconscious animal soldiers woke from their deep sleep and rubbed their eyes, their wounds miraculously healed. Cries of "Victory to Hanuman! Victory to Hanuman!" filled the air.

"The whole universe is grateful to you, Hanuman. Thank you for saving our lives!" said Ram.

Now that the animal soldiers were revived, Ram's army advanced once again on the battlefield and the tide turned quickly in their favor. It was Lakshman who struck the deciding blow. Using a sacred weapon given to him by Lord Indra, he released a razor sharp arrow that killed Ravana's son, Indrajeet.

Ravana roared in anger and sorrow at the loss of his son, but he was far too arrogant and stubborn to surrender. Instead, he chose to duel with Ram. It would be his last battle. After hours of hard combat, Ram aimed a fatal arrow at Ravana's navel and the evil demon's spirit floated away. Finally, the world was freed from Ravana's tyranny. As he had been warned so often, Ravana paid with his life for stealing Sita from Ram.

The noble Prince Vibhishana became the new King of Lanka, and after the coronation he accompanied Ram, Sita, Lakshman, and their army of monkeys on a ride in the flying Pushpaka chariot. In the twinkling of an eye, they reached the kingdom of Ayodhya.

Ram's return to Ayodhya marked the end of a long exile. He had left the kingdom to honor his father's promise: though Ram was the rightful heir, King Dasharatha had decreed that Ram's brother Bharat should rule Ayodhya first. In the fourteen years that Ram spent wandering the earth, he had cleared the world of countless cruel and deceitful demons. He had done well, but oh, how good it felt to come home at last!

In a splendid and elaborate ceremony, Ram was crowned King of Ayodhya. On this happy occasion, everyone received gifts. "I would never have found Sita without your help," Ram said to Hanuman, handing him a long, gleaming necklace. "Will this string of pearls please your heart?"

A while later King Vibhishana spotted Hanuman sitting by himself, popping the pearls into his mouth and crunching them up into little shards. "What are you doing? You shouldn't eat pearls. Spit them out! Don't you know how precious they are?" cried Vibhishana.

"They have no value for me. They do not bear Ram's name," said Hanuman.

"What do you mean? You don't bear Ram's name either—does that mean you, too, are without value?" teased Vibhishana.

Hanuman looked up. Wordlessly, he split open his own chest with his sharp nails. An image of Ram, Sita, and Lakshman glowed in the center of his heart and the name "Ram" appeared on his body, written over and over again.

Vibhishana fell to his knees in awe. Ram hurried to Hanuman's side, closed the wound with the touch of his fingers, and then embraced the monkey.

"What a truly precious monkey you are! What a wise, courageous, and perfect monkey! Here. Leave these pearls, and take my signet ring instead." Ram slipped his gold signet ring onto Hanuman's finger. "As long as you live on Earth, always be sure to help the meek and innocent."

"Yes my Lord, I will," Hanuman promised and kissed the inscription on the ring—*Ram, Ram, Ram.*

Hanuman has kept his promise to this very day. And he will continue to keep it as long as people recite the Ramayana to remember Ram's story.

Note to Parents and Teachers

The story of Hanuman, taken from the Valmiki Ramayana, has inspired Indian children and adults alike for thousands of years. It is my hope that this version of the story, retold for American children, will inspire them as well. In India, people revere Hanuman as a positive role model. He is intelligent and clever, powerful and strong, and possesses many magical abilities. With all of these gifts comes responsibility. Hanuman has to make choices: He could side with Vali, the wicked monkey king, or with the good king, Sugriva, whom Vali has deposed. He could side with Ravana, the wicked demon king, or with the virtuous Lord Ram, who has accepted exile to honor a promise made by his father. Hanuman always chooses to side with the good. In his humility and sincere desire to help those who tell the truth, Hanuman uses his gifts wisely. Hanuman's story is meant to encourage children to make good use of their own gifts—to speak up and stand fearlessly against injustice, cruelty, tyranny, and oppression, just as Hanuman stood fearlessly against Ravana's army of ruthless demons.

The
Magical Adventures
of Krishna

How a Mischief Maker
Saved the World

Vatsala Sperling

Illustrated by Pieter Weltevrede

About Krishna

The Hindu people from India believe that whenever the earth is taken over by evil, the prayers of the weak will be heard by Lords Brahma, Vishnu, and Shiva (gods of creation, preservation, and destruction, respectively). Then the gods will work together to restore order and peace.

An ancient text in the Sanskrit language, the Srimad Bhagavatam, describes one such event from thousands of years ago. It tells the story of a time when demons ruled the world, led by the evil demon king Kansa. The gods decided that Vishnu should go to Earth to defeat Kansa and his cronies.

So Vishnu was born on Earth as a baby boy named Krishna. In his childhood, Krishna was a fun-loving and curious boy. He loved to play tricks on the village milkmaids, stealing the butter pots right off their heads. And he played the flute so beautifully that he enchanted all who heard him. But as carefree and childish as he seemed, Krishna was always on the lookout for demons, bravely killing any that crossed his path.

Whatever he did, Krishna acted with such flair, charm, playfulness, and humor that the stories of his many adventures continue to entertain and inspire us even today.

The northern plains of India, below the majestic Himalaya Mountains, were very fertile at one time. The great river Yamuna began her journey in the icy peaks of the Himalayas and ran through the northern plains on her way to the ocean, nourishing the soil as she flowed. On the banks of the Yamuna, several villages nestled in an endless expanse of wild, green woods and lush, rolling meadows. Amid such beauty and splendor, the citizens of Mathura herded cattle and lived quite prosperously.

But everything changed when the demon Kansa became king of Mathura. Kansa commanded a great empire, but he ruled his subjects with an iron fist and evil intentions. His greed for wealth was insatiable. To fill his royal coffers, he taxed the poor villagers very harshly. When people could not pay up, he sent his fierce demon messengers to punish them. Wherever these demons went, chaos and destruction followed. They demolished whole villages, killed children, stole cattle, and set fire to standing crops. They stopped at nothing, and the people got the message loud and clear: "Pay your taxes or else!"

It soon became impossible for people to keep up with the unjust demands of their cruel king. They knew that Kansa had imprisoned his own father, the kind and generous king Ugrasena, simply because the old king had objected to his son's ruthless greed. The people had no one to turn to. In desperation, they looked to the heavens and prayed to Lord Vishnu, saying, "Please help us, Narayana."

Another cry for help to the people came from the earth goddess, Bhumi. Bhumi was very generous. She gave her rich soil and flowing waters freely so that all the people could prosper. But no matter how she tried, Bhumi could not produce enough wealth to satisfy Kansa's greed. She knew that the people lived in terror of their king. No matter how hard they worked, they could never fill Kansa's bottomless coffers. Bhumi felt helpless as she watched the innocent people suffer. When she could bear no more, she took the form of a cow and went to the heavens to seek help from Lords Brahma and Shiva. Lord Brahma had created Kansa. Lord Shiva would know how to destroy him. The gods listened to Bhumi's tale of woe. After some deep thinking, they said, "Only Narayana can help in these hard times, Bhumi. Let's go see him."

Soon they arrived at Lord Vishnu's home in the Ksheer Sagar, an ocean of milk that nourished the entire creation. Vishnu bobbed gently on the waves of milk, resting on the back of his great serpent, Shesha. The five-headed serpent made a magnificent coil and spread out his hoods. His ten beady eyes shone like jewels and five red tongues leaped out of his mouths like flames from a roaring fire pit. Lord Vishnu's wife, the goddess Lakshmi, sat beside him on the serpent's back.

Bhumi bowed humbly to Lord Vishnu. "Help us, Narayana," she cried. "Kansa, the cruel demon king, has made life impossible for the people. No one feels safe anymore." Bhumi's eyes stung with hot tears and her voice quavered as she begged for Lord Vishnu's help on Earth.

"Don't worry," he comforted Bhumi. "I will be born on Earth as Krishna to teach those demons a lesson." Patting Shesha, Vishnu said, "On Earth, you will be my cousin Balaram." Then he winked at his wife and said, "Sweetheart, I cannot live without you. You will be my girlfriend, Radha."

Bhumi sighed with relief, because she knew that Lord Vishnu would keep his word.

In the whole world, the one person Kansa loved dearly was his little sister, Princess Devaki. He had just attended Devaki's marriage to Vasudeva, the king of a clan of cowherds. After the wedding, Kansa drove the newlyweds' chariot, whistling a merry tune and urging the handsome horses on. The starry-eyed couple waved to the people who had come out in droves to greet them. All of a sudden, a booming voice spoke from the sky. "Beware, Kansa! Your dear sister, Devaki, will have eight sons and the eighth will be the death of you."

A hush fell over the jubilant crowd. Kansa's face froze. He looked around. Raising his proud head to the heavens, he said in a voice as loud and booming as the voice from above, "There will be no Devaki! She will have no eighth son!"

In a flash, he jumped out of the chariot. His cruel, steely eyes blazed bloodred as he grabbed Devaki by her long hair, dragged her out of the chariot, and took a sword to her neck.

Vasudeva was horrified. He cried, "O King, is this any way to treat your dear sister on her wedding day? She is innocent. Let her go! I promise that I will give you our eighth child."

Kansa knew that Vasudeva would keep his word. He let go of Devaki and sheathed his sword. But instead of driving the newlyweds to their royal palace, he locked them up in a fortress dungeon on the banks of the Yamuna River. His father, King Ugrasena, was jailed there as well.

There is really no need to kill my beloved little sister, thought Kansa. *But her eighth child will not live to see the light of day! Anyway, I'm safe until she delivers her eighth son.*

In due time Kansa learned that Devaki had given birth to her first baby boy. He thought nothing of it. But Sage Narada, a holy man devoted to Lord Vishnu, visited Kansa's palace soon after the baby was born. He held a lotus flower in his hand. "Look at this flower, Kansa. Tell me which is the first petal and which is the eighth?" he asked with a sly grin.

Kansa thought for a moment. He knew that Sage Narada's questions always pointed to a hidden meaning. Something clicked in

Kansa's devious mind. He threw the flower down and marched straight into Devaki's prison cell. Snatching the baby from her lap, he flung the child against the wall, killing him instantly. Devaki fainted and fell to the floor, while Vasudeva looked on, frozen in horror. "You must give me all of your sons, not just the eighth one," Kansa ordered Vasudeva. He turned on his heel and marched out of the prison.

Sage Narada saw it all, and smiled knowingly. He knew that Lord Vishnu had seen everything too. The crueler Kansa became, the sooner Lord Vishnu would come to Earth.

Every year Devaki gave birth to a baby boy. Every baby met his end soon after he was born. Devaki's tears had dried up. She lived in a daze. With each and every breath she prayed, "Please help us, Narayana."

Lord Vishnu heard each of her prayers. When he felt that Devaki could hold on no longer, he summoned Yogamaya, the goddess of illusion. "I am going to Earth to be born as Devaki's eighth son. I need you to come to Earth, too, to help me play a trick on Kansa. Go to the home of Nanda and Yashoda on the banks of the Yamuna River and take birth as their baby girl."

Yogamaya knew to say, "Yes, Sir."

It was the eighth night after the dark moon in the month of August. Monsoon rains had just begun on the plains of northern India. The night sky, dark as ink and laden with black, ominous clouds, was lit every now and then with a bright, blinding streak of lightning. Rolling thunder made it impossible to hear anything. Throughout the day and night rains had come in great torrents, causing flash floods in the city of Mathura and swelling the river Yamuna where it flowed just outside the prison gates. The night was scary and dark. The river was deep and wild.

Within the prison walls, Devaki gave birth to her eighth son. She named him Krishna for he was as dark as the night outside. She raised the newborn to her lips to kiss him before Kansa took him away. Just then she noticed something strange—a halo around the baby's head! She whispered to Vasudeva, "Look! Look at our baby . . ." and they saw that in his tiny hands the baby held a little conch shell, a mace, a discus, and a lotus flower—the four sacred objects of Lord Vishnu! They wondered aloud, "Could our baby be Lord Vishnu?"

In answer, the baby spoke. "Mother, Father, this is not the first time I have come to Earth, and it will not be the last. I come to protect the innocent every time the earth is taken over by evil. Quickly now, take me to Nanda and Yashoda's home. They will raise me as their own. And bring their daughter back with you."

The next moment, the four sacred objects disappeared from the baby's hands and he became a helpless newborn again, squirming to find his thumb. Vasudeva noticed that his shackles had fallen to the floor. The lock on the gate had broken open, as if by magic, and the guards had fallen sound asleep. Quickly, he gathered some rags, wrapped the baby snugly, laid him in a basket, and stepped outside.

Vasudeva knew that Nanda and his wife, Yashoda, lived in Gokul, a little village just across the river from the prison, but to get there he had to cross the raging floodwaters. "Help me please, Narayana," he said as he stepped into the river, holding the baby high above his head. The water flowed right up to his chin and he struggled against the powerful current. But just then the river water touched one of Krishna's tiny toes and immediately the flood began to subside. A clear path opened up right in front of Vasudeva and a snake came slithering behind him, spreading its mighty hood over the baby to protect him from the downpour.

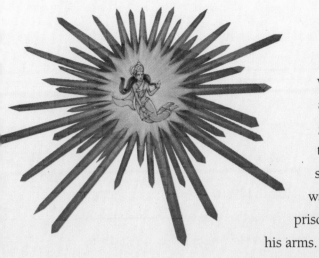

In Nanda's house, his wife, Yashoda, was fast asleep after giving birth to a baby girl. Very quietly, Vasudeva tiptoed to Yashoda's bedside, swapped the babies, and walked all the way back to the prison, cradling her daughter in his arms.

In the morning Kansa got news of the birth. *I will waste no time in getting rid of the baby,* he thought, and he marched right over to Devaki's cell.

"Please spare this one child, Brother, she's a little girl!" cried Devaki. Kansa hesitated for a moment. *Maybe there's nothing to the prediction,* he thought. *The eighth child is supposed to be a boy . . .* Then fearing some trick, he roughly snatched the baby from his sister's frail arms. But as he tried to fling her against the wall, the baby girl slipped right out of Kansa's hands. She floated to a high spot on the ceiling beyond his reach and said, "Kansa, your killer is in Gokul." Startled, Kansa looked up and saw that the baby was none other than Yogamaya, who had disguised herself as the fearsome goddess Durga to give him a really good scare. Pale and shaken, he fled from the cell.

In Gokul, Nanda and Yashoda woke up in the morning and saw an unusually dark-skinned baby boy in their bed. "I thought I had given birth to a baby girl," Yashoda said to herself. But the next moment her doubt had vanished and she was flooded with an immense feeling of love for her new baby boy.

Little Krishna grew to be an adorable child, always smiling and gurgling and growing stronger every day. Yashoda loved to carry him on her hip while she did her chores. But one day as she swept the courtyard she said, "Either you are the heaviest baby on Earth or I am getting weak." She laid Krishna down to rest her weary back.

At that very moment a dust storm blew into the village. Dust stung Yashoda's eyes and blinded her. She groped around but could not find Krishna. She called out to him, but her voice was lost in the deafening roar of the storm.

This storm was actually the demon Trinavrata. Kansa had sent him to Gokul to find and kill Krishna. When he spotted the baby in Yashoda's courtyard he scooped him up and said, "Care to come for a ride, sonny?"

Krishna never refused a chance for fun. He flew happily into the sky on the spinning cloud of dust. But soon, just like Yashoda, the weary demon began to mumble, "Either you are the heaviest baby on Earth or I am getting weak." Krishna continued to grow heavier and heavier. Trinavrata could not carry him anymore, but Krishna would not let go. Holding fast to the demon's dusty beard, he said, "I am going down and you are going down with me, Trinavrata." Soon they both came tumbling from the dusty sky.

When the storm ended, a worried Yashoda called out, "Krishna, where are you?" She heard Krishna's joyful squeals and found him well and happy, exactly where she had left him just a few moments before. But next to him was the shattered body of a demon!

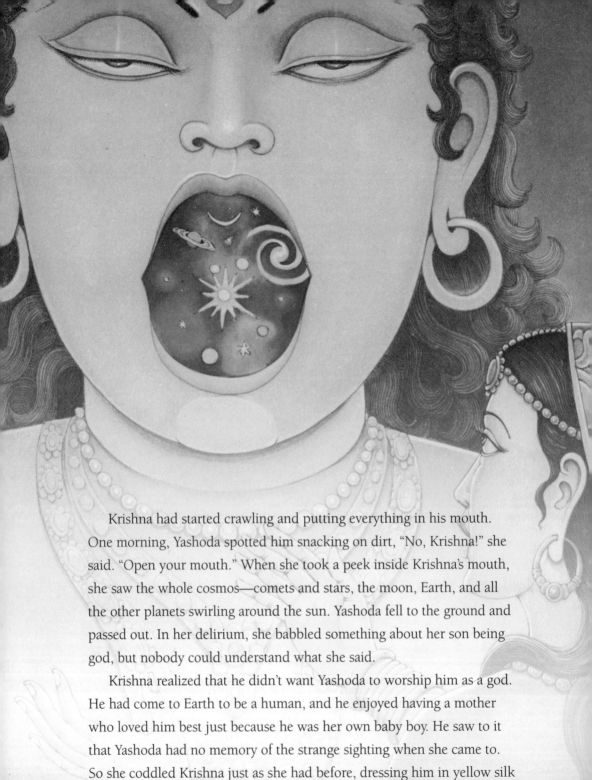

Krishna had started crawling and putting everything in his mouth.
One morning, Yashoda spotted him snacking on dirt, "No, Krishna!" she
said. "Open your mouth." When she took a peek inside Krishna's mouth,
she saw the whole cosmos—comets and stars, the moon, Earth, and all
the other planets swirling around the sun. Yashoda fell to the ground and
passed out. In her delirium, she babbled something about her son being
god, but nobody could understand what she said.

Krishna realized that he didn't want Yashoda to worship him as a god.
He had come to Earth to be a human, and he enjoyed having a mother
who loved him best just because he was her own baby boy. He saw to it
that Yashoda had no memory of the strange sighting when she came to.
So she coddled Krishna just as she had before, dressing him in yellow silk
and tucking a peacock feather into his curly locks. The brilliant rainbow
colors of the feather looked beautiful against Krishna's dark, glowing skin.

When he was just a little boy, Krishna's family moved from Gokul to the village of Vrindavan. When he grew a little older, Krishna joined the other village boys as they herded the cows out to pasture. As a toddler, he had developed a taste for fresh butter. Now he organized butter-stealing parties with his cowherd friends. Krishna and company would sneak into their neighbors' larders and help themselves to as much butter as they could eat.

The distraught neighbors came to Yashoda with their complaints.

"Your Krishna is a thief. He steals our butter and disappears."

"And he makes our cows disappear at milking time!"

"You must punish him, Yashoda. Do something!"

Yashoda tried to speak sternly to Krishna. But he would put on such an innocent smile and speak with such charm that she couldn't stay angry for long. When Krishna gave his mother an affectionate bear hug and protested, "Mother, you love me. You know I don't steal . . ." all of Yashoda's doubts and anger would fall from her like dry, old leaves from the trees. No complaint could make Yashoda love Krishna any less.

Soon, however, Krishna's fun with butter began costing the villagers their livelihoods. Every week they carried pots of butter on their heads to pay the tax collectors across the river in Mathura. But the tax collectors got nothing when Krishna and his friends hid in the trees and stole the butter pots right off the milkmaids' heads. The villagers complained to Kansa that Krishna ate up all their butter. Of course, that made Kansa furious. He turned to his demon crony Vatasura and ordered him to kill Krishna, exclaiming, "That boy must die!"

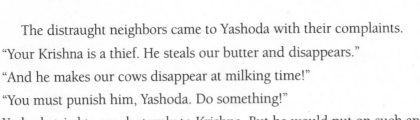

Vatasura turned himself into a calf and joined Krishna's herd. *When Krishna comes to pet me I will make a pulp out of him,* he thought. But Krishna noticed that one of the calves looked a bit too perfect, yet none of the cows would let him suckle. Curious, Krishna approached the calf and asked him, "Where is your mother?" The calf was waiting for just this moment. His features began to harden and he growled at Krishna. In a flash, Krishna grabbed the calf by his tail, spun him around above his head, and threw him up into the sky beyond the tree line. The calf landed with a thud among rocks and shrubs. He was no longer a cute little calf. Now he was a dead demon.

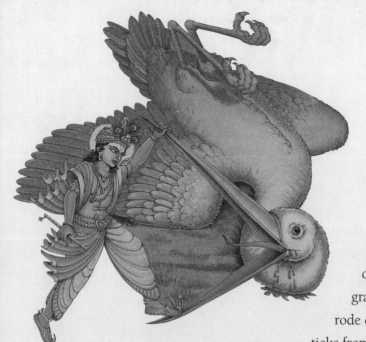

Next, Kansa sent the demon Bakasura to finish off Krishna. *I will make mincemeat out of Krishna with my sharp talons and beak,* thought Bakasura as he turned himself into a bird and landed on the back of one of Krishna's cows. The cows grazed peacefully. A few birds rode on their backs, picking out ticks from time to time. But Krishna spotted a bird that seemed to be a little bit too alert, as if it was looking for someone. "Looks like you are from a different flock," Krishna said, and gently he lifted the bird off the cow's back. The demon bird was waiting for just this moment. He began pecking furiously at Krishna. Poor bird. Soon, his sharp beak was forced apart and instead of a bird, there lay Bakasura meeting his maker.

The demon Aghasura was full of rage. He wanted to avenge the death of his brother, Bakasura. "I will eat Krishna alive," he promised Kansa, and he turned himself into a huge serpent. With his mouth wide open, he lay coiled in the path that Krishna took when he herded his cows back to the village.

"You guys stay here. I need to see about this snake," Krishna said to his friends as he marched gallantly into the serpent's gaping mouth. As Krishna ventured farther in, the serpent's long stomach got narrower and narrower. "Okay, it's time for me to grow up," said Krishna, and he began to grow bigger and bigger and bigger, stretching the serpent's belly until it could stretch no more. Krishna's friends heard a noise that sounded as if the earth itself was tearing apart . . . and out from the torn flesh of the serpent stepped a smiling Krishna.

The story of
Krishna's brave
encounters with
the demons made
all of the young
milkmaids fall in
love with him.
Each of them
wanted Krishna
for her husband.
One day while
the milkmaids were
bathing in the river, Krishna
happened to pass by. He spotted
their clothes lying on the riverbank. Scooping them up, he climbed to
the highest branch of a nearby tree and began playing his flute. When
the girls heard his music, they wanted to come out of the river to meet
him. But when they looked up, they saw their clothes hanging from the
highest branches of the tree!

"Give us our clothes, Krishna," they begged.

"Come out of the river and get them," teased Krishna.

One by one, the girls came out of the river, covering
themselves with their hands as best as they
could. Krishna cast a kind gaze upon each
of them. As if by magic, the girls felt
free of their romantic designs on
Krishna. Now they felt only divine
love in their hearts. "You are our
lord," they said. Krishna was
very, very happy to be out
from under so many marriage
proposals.

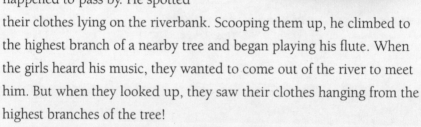

Though naughty and full of mischief, Krishna was also very good at understanding how the human heart yearns for love. On one full-moon night, he began playing his flute. His divine music wafted into every home on the soft, floral-scented breeze, and from every home, out came the milkmaids. Tall and short, fat and thin, beautiful and ugly, dark and fair—not one of them could resist Krishna's enchanting music. Entranced, they made a beeline for the source of the melody. Soon every milkmaid found herself facing her very own Krishna, for Krishna had multiplied himself into many. "I am everywhere," he said. "To experience me, all you have to do is awaken pure love in your heart."

There was not a cloud in the sky. The milkmaids and Krishna danced and danced all night long, the moon shining brightly on their lovely faces. The rhythmic tapping of their feet and the rustling of their silky robes were the only other sounds besides the melody from Krishna's flute.

The real Krishna played and danced with his eternal sweetheart, Radha, just as he had promised Goddess Lakshmi in the Ksheer Sagar. Into her ear he whispered, "As long as the sun and the moon appear in the sky, our names will be chanted together."

It was a custom in those days, as the hot summer months were coming to an end, to pray to Lord Indra, ruler of the heavens and dispenser of rain, for life-giving rains to nourish the crops. It had not rained in a long time. The Yamuna River was running low. In places, the riverbed was dry. The cows grew thin and gaunt with no fresh grass to eat. But still, Lord Indra did not send the rains.

Krishna said, "The rains will come when the clouds have gathered enough water. Instead of flattering Indra, let us honor the wise men of our community." Lord Indra did not like all attention diverted from him. In a fury he sent a searing bolt of lightning followed by rain so hard it could peel skin off the body.

The villagers panicked, "O Narayana, save us from Lord Indra," they prayed. Krishna was none other than Narayana, and he always heard a call for help. He lifted Govardhan Mountain on his little pinky and held it up like an umbrella. The cattle and the villagers took shelter under the mountain. The battering rains continued on, but now no one cared. Humbled, Lord Indra appeared before Krishna and said, "Forgive me, Narayana." The rains became gentle and soft, and the happy villagers returned to their homes.

Kansa's demons had made many attempts on Krishna's life, but Krishna had killed them all without suffering so much as a scratch. This made Kansa very unhappy. He summoned Akrura, a great devotee of Lord Vishnu. "Akrura, my friend," said Kansa, "I regret that for years I have tried to kill my nephew Krishna. I would like to meet him. Please bring him here."

Akrura doubted Kansa's intentions, but he hitched two handsome horses to his wagon and headed toward Gokul, praying all the way, "Help us, Narayana." The villagers said, "Your cousin Balaram will go with you, Krishna. We will not let you go alone."

On the way to Mathura, the horses needed a drink. "Water the horses. We will wait in the carriage," Krishna said. Akrura watered the horses and hitched them back up. When he returned to the lake for a cooling swim, he saw an image in the water—Krishna reclined on a coiled serpent, holding a conch shell, a mace, a lotus flower, and a discus in his hands. Akrura couldn't believe his eyes. He looked back at the wagon on the shore. Krishna and Balaram were sitting right where he had left them! He swam back to the shore and fell at Krishna's feet, crying, "You are Narayana, aren't you?"

"You must be seeing things," said Krishna. He hugged Akrura, and the devotee's heart filled with hope and love.

In Mathura, Kansa received Krishna and Balaram very warmly. He led the boys into a public arena and announced to the crowd, "Now, my nephews will play with elephants!" Kansa hoped that the elephants would crush the boys to death. But, the boys flattened the charging beasts as if they were children's toys. Pulling off the tusks, they waved to the cheering crowds.

Not one to give up, Kansa cried, "Krishna and Balaram will now take on my wrestlers!"

"Only two against so many . . . not fair," murmured the crowd. But Kansa ignored their protests and signaled for his bloodthirsty wrestlers to attack the boys. Krishna and Balaram slew the wrestlers in a matter of minutes. Humiliated, Kansa called his eight brothers for help. Again, Krishna and Balaram killed them with one sweep of their hands.

There was no one left on Kansa's side. "Well, *I* will crush these boys like bugs," he boasted, as he marched into the ring.

"You can deal with him, Krishna," said Balaram. He stood aside as Krishna gathered Kansa's hair in his hand, pulled his uncle's head back, and struck one fatal blow to his spine. The crowd could not believe that the reign of terror was over! They spilled over into the ring, lifted the boys onto their shoulders, and danced with joy.

The earth goddess, Bhumi, sighed with relief. "Thank you, Narayana, for fulfilling your promise," she said with gratitude.

Soon after, Krishna and Balaram headed to the prison to meet with Devaki, Vasudeva, and King Ugrasena. Krishna's parents hugged him with joy.

To the late Kansa's father, Krishna said, "Grandfather, now you'll have a chance to undo all of Kansa's evil deeds."

"I am old, my child," said Ugrasena. "You deserve to be the king."

"Not me!" cried Krishna. "I'd rather herd my beloved cows than be a king and live in a palace." Once Grandfather Ugrasena was crowned and Krishna's parents had been set free, Krishna and Balaram returned to Gokul.

Krishna could escape being a king for the time being, but he could not escape going to school. He was sent to the ashram of Rishi Sandeepani, where he spent years learning how to become a warrior king. All that training would help him keep his promise to mankind, "Anytime the earth is overrun with evil, I will come to restore peace and order."

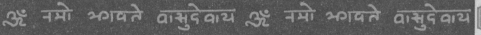

A Note to Parents and Teachers

At its heart, Krishna's story is the story of a child wanting pure love from his mother. Though he is a divine incarnation, born with unparalleled strength and magical powers, he doesn't want to be worshipped as a god. He wants only to be loved as a human child. His story points to the primal need of all children. Receiving love from parents and community is a child's birthright. When given unconditionally, it allows the child to develop his or her true potential as an adult.

The Hindu worldview recognizes nine primary emotional states, or *rasas*. They are both positive and negative, ranging from love, bravery, and tranquillity to fear, disgust, and anger. In India small children are encouraged to express the full range of emotions in order to become fully developed human beings. Small children are considered innocent, even godlike, so even their negative emotional expressions are seen only as opportunities to give them the love they need. An Indian mother will call her child "Krishna" as a reminder that innocence and trust are the true powers that children bring into the world.

Who Is the Greatest Archer in the World: Karna or Arjuna?

Vatsala Sperling

Illustrated by Sandeep Johari,
Nona Weltevrede, and Pieter Weltevrede

About Karna and Arjuna

The Mahabharata, a grand epic from ancient India, tells of a war between two branches of a royal family—the Pandavas and the Kauravas. The Pandavas represent the forces of good, while the Kauravas represent the darker side of human nature. Two characters in this epic—Karna and Arjuna— are brothers, although they don't know it. Both are Queen Kunti's sons, given to her by the gods in response to her chanting of a secret mantra. Arjuna is one of the five Pandava princes, given to Queen Kunti and her husband, King Pandu. But Kunti received Karna from the Sun God when she recited the mantra as a curious twelve-year-old girl. Dismayed, she gave him up at birth, and he has been raised by a poor charioteer and his wife. He knows nothing of his royal heritage.

Karna and Arjuna have each nurtured a lifelong ambition to be known as the best archer in the world. Though Karna's humble upbringing has denied him an opportunity to compete against the princely Arjuna in a public archery contest, the Mahabharata battlefield brings these two brothers and arch enemies face-to-face. Publicly shunned by the royal Pandava brothers, Karna has been befriended by their evil Kaurava cousin Duryodhana. Loyal to his friend to the end, he has no choice but to take Duryodhana's side in the war, even though he knows it's the wrong side. Meanwhile, Arjuna, a kind and gentle soul, would rather not fight in the war at all until Krishna (an earthly form of Vishnu, God of Preservation) helps him see that he was born to fight for the forces of good. This is his dharma—his divine destiny. In the end, Arjuna wins the war, but he bows to his fallen brother Karna, declaring him to be the best archer in the world.

A long time ago, a beautiful young princess named Kunti lived with her uncle, King Kuntibhoj, in a lovely palace along the banks of a wide river. One day, when she was just twelve years old, her uncle said to her, "Kunti, an important visitor will be arriving soon. Sage Durvasa is very learned and we are honored to receive him as our royal guest, but he is well known for his terrible temper. Child, I am asking you to make sure that all his needs are met. Give him no reason at all to become angry. Please do be careful, Kunti, the future of my kingdom depends on you. Sage Durvasa has the power to put terrible curses on anyone who displeases him!"

"Yes, Uncle," Kunti promised, and soon she turned herself into a most perfect hostess. She could almost read Sage Durvasa's mind and met his every need before he realized anything was wanting. The sage had a very peaceful and happy stay and wanted to reward Kunti for her services. He studied her face and used his magic powers to see into her future. "Child," he said, "one day you will need help from the gods. I am going to teach you a secret mantra for inviting the gods into your life. Be very careful with this mantra! Use it wisely." Kunti repeated the syllables after him. She promised to use the mantra only in times of great need.

But Kunti was only twelve, after all, and she was a lively and curious girl! Early the next morning she was playing by herself in the royal garden. The sun had risen and Kunti watched as its rays touched a flower here, a leaf there. She felt its warmth on her skin. She thought about the Sun God waking up the whole world. *I wonder . . . she* thought. *I wonder if the Sun would come to me.* Forgetting her promise to Sage Durvasa, she began to recite the mantra. She closed her eyes and concentrated the way she had been taught. Soon her body became prickly hot, as if she was sitting by a fire. She could hear the fire roar and crackle! She opened her eyes to see a glowing chariot swooping down from the heavens. It was pulled by seven horses—and the Sun God himself was driving them! "You called me," Sun said, stepping from the carriage with a baby in his arms. "You called me," he said again, placing the baby in her lap, "and I bring you my son."

Kunti looked at the baby. *Oh no!* She thought. *What have I done?* "Sun," she wailed. "I am only twelve years old! I didn't know what I was doing. Please! Take your baby away! Her cries mingled with the cries of the infant in her lap. "Please! I am not ready to be a mother!"

"You used the sacred mantra," the Sun God replied. "The baby is your responsibility now. But I leave him with divine gifts. Look—he has a pair of golden earrings and he wears a golden shield on his chest. They will grow with him. As long as he wears them, he cannot be killed." The Sun God sped off into the morning sky, leaving poor Kunti alone with a newborn babe in her arms.

She was panic-stricken. What a string of curses Sage Durvasa would hurl at her now! She would live in shame! Who would ever believe that the Sun God had brought her a child? Then she looked again at the baby, squirming in her arms, shimmering with celestial light just like his father. She rocked him gently. His cries quieted, and Kunti realized that she had stopped crying too. "Alas, I cannot be your mother," she said sadly. "I am much too young. I will have to let you go."

Kunti found a sturdy
basket, some wax, and
cloth of the softest silk.
She coated the basket
with the wax to make
it waterproof and lined
it with layers of silk
to make it soft and
warm. She placed the
baby carefully in his
new bed and carried the
basket to the river. Then
she kissed him good-bye and
set the basket afloat. "Farewell,"
she whispered, "may the Sun God watch
over you and always keep you safe. May you find parents who will love
you and care for you. I will always remember you." Drying her tears as
best she could, she walked slowly back to the palace.

The tiny basket bounced up and down in the current, but Kunti
had made it well, and the baby never even got wet. Sun hovered above
and cloaked himself in a veil of clouds so as not to melt the wax of the
basket—though every now and then he sent down a ray or two to keep
the baby nice and warm.

Downstream, Adhiratha was sitting on a rock, hoping to catch a fish
for the midday meal. He was a gentle and good man, a charioteer by
trade, and his wife, Radha, was a gentle and good woman. They were
often sad, however, for they were unable to have children. How they
longed for a baby of their own! Adhiratha sighed as he thought about
their lonely life. He cast the line out over the river and sighed again.
But what was that at the bend in the river, illuminated by a single ray

peeking through the clouds? Adhiratha waded out into the current and caught hold of the basket. When he saw its precious cargo he was at a complete loss for words. "Oh!" he gasped as he ran all the way home, carrying the basket in his arms. "Oh!" he gasped as he stood dripping in the doorway, holding the basket out for his dear wife to see. When Radha saw the tiny baby lying peacefully asleep, his earrings and shield glowing like golden flames, she was speechless too. "Oh! Oh! Oh!" she gasped. When the baby woke up and gave a little cry, Radha's breast filled with milk as if by magic. She picked up the baby and let him nurse to his heart's content. Finally, she found just the right words, "Our son is beautiful!" she said.

Born to a princess and the Sun God, this baby was half royal and half divine, and he was indeed a beautiful child. Adhiratha and Radha did not know his origin but they adored him just the same. The couple named their new son Vasushena, which means "born with shield and earrings," and they raised him as their own. Adhiratha and Radha considered themselves blessed, and the three made a very happy family. Their small cottage was richer than the largest palace of the kingdom, for within its humble walls this cottage held love. Later Vasushena came to be known as Karna, and so we shall call him Karna as his story continues.

Years passed. As Karna grew to be a sweet and energetic little boy, Kunti became a graceful young woman and married King Pandu of Hastinapur. In days of old, Indian kings could marry more than one wife. Along with Kunti, Pandu married another princess named Madri. Before the newlyweds could settle down together, however, King Pandu set off to fight a war against the neighboring kingdoms. When he returned from the war, Pandu was tired and wanted to go to the forest to rest with his wives for a while. He asked his blind older brother, Dhritrashtra, to rule in his place during his absence. Dhritrashtra's wife, Gandhari, would be queen. Gandhari had good vision, but she always wore a blindfold, refusing to see the world that her husband could not see. Dhritrashtra happily agreed to become king. Secretly, he hoped that Pandu would stay away forever. He wanted one of his own sons to inherit the throne.

King Pandu and his wives lived a tranquil life together in the forest, but alas, their bliss was short lived. While out hunting one morning, King Pandu took aim at a pair of deer, killing the doe. Unbeknownst to the king, the two deer were actually a sage and his wife in disguise. Horrified, Pandu watched as the doe changed into the body of a dead woman, while her mate transformed into the figure of a sage. "I am so sorry! I am so terribly sorry!" Pandu kept saying. But the sage was distraught with grief and cursed Pandu. "I will never again feel my wife's tender embrace," he said. "As punishment, the moment you embrace your wives, you, too, will die!"

Pandu told Kunti and Madri the terrible news. "I love you both, but I can never touch you," he said. "We will never have children together!"

Kunti was quiet for a while, remembering the Sun God swooping down from the sky with a baby in his arms. She thought to herself, *this time I am ready to care for a baby.* She told Pandu about the secret mantra for inviting the gods, and he readily agreed to let her try it. Kunti used the mantra to summon Dharmaraj, Lord of Dharma and Justice, who gave her a son, Yudhisthira. After some time, Kunti summoned Pavan, the mighty god of wind, and he gave her a son, Bhima.

A few years later, Pandu said to Kunti, "Let us have another child." Please use your sacred mantra again." Kunti whispered the sacred mantra inviting Indra, God of Thunderstorms, and with a bolt of lightning, a beautiful baby boy appeared in her lap. A booming voice filled the air— the voice of Indra himself! "This is Arjuna, my son. He will grow strong and fearless and will conquer the forces of evil!"

Pandu and Kunti were delighted with their handsome new baby. And Kunti taught the mantra to Madri as well, who received two more sons for King Pandu—the twins Nakula and Sahadeva—from Ashwini, God of Beauty and Grace. The five boys grew strong and brave and courteous. They became known as the Pandava brothers. Venerable sages taught them the sacred texts and the god-given laws of dharma so that they would become wise rulers. Knowing that the brothers were destined to fight the forces of evil, the sages also gave them lessons in weaponry and military strategy. Arjuna in particular showed an early talent and passion for archery.

Kunti adored her five sons, but she had long kept a secret from Pandu. She had never told him about the son she had given away when she was twelve. After setting that child afloat in a river, she had always wondered and worried about him. For now, however, she was the happy mother of five beautiful boys.

Meanwhile, in the palace of Hastinapur, Dhritrashtra's wife, Queen Gandhari, also became pregnant. Her pregnancy, however, lasted for two long years. When she gave birth, it was not to a baby but rather to a strange round object that was as hard as iron and as hot as burning coal. She lamented bitterly, sure that she would never bear a child. Dhritrashtra's grandfather, Sage Vyasa, heard Gandhari weeping and came to console her.

"I can help," he said. "Don't worry." In a secret chamber, he filled 101 earthen pots with a magic potion. Then he broke the strange object into 101 pieces and dropped them one by one into the pots. He covered the pots with tight lids and instructed that no one should disturb the pots, lift up the lids, or even step into the secret chamber for the next two years.

Two years later, hearing a huge commotion, Gandhari; Dhritrashtra; his younger brother, Vidur; and the grandfather of the entire clan, Bhishma, rushed into the secret chamber. The pots were rolling and crashing about and the air was filled with sounds of whimpering and cooing. Because of her blindfold, Gandhari could not see the source of all the uproar. But imagine her joy when Grandfather Bhishma told her that the room held one hundred baby boys and one baby girl, with the drops of magic potion still glistening on their soft skin! He congratulated Dhirtrashtra and Gandhari on continuing the lineage of their ancestor Kuru by becoming parents to these 101 children—all members of the Kaurava clan.

Then one of the babies started to scream, his face twisted with rage. Red sparks flew from his eyes and ears and mouth. Black crows circled above his broken pot and wolves licked their chops nearby. Grandfather Bhishma knew that wolves and crows were bad omens. He warned Gandhari and Dhritrashtra, saying, "You must send this one away to Grandfather Vyasa. He will know how to raise him well."

But the king and queen ignored his advice. The baby seemed strong! Surely he would be the one to inherit the throne. They named him Duryodhana and lavished him with attention. "Duryodhana is our crown prince," Dhritrashtra said. "We will keep him."

As Bhishma feared, Duryodhana proved to be a nasty little boy. He wrapped his parents around his little finger, while they spoiled him shamelessly. When he got his own way, he seemed nice enough, but woe to anyone who crossed him! All the maids and servants, and his ninety-nine brothers and one sister, lived in fear of his cruel tricks.

In contrast, the Pandava brothers lived in harmony. The younger boys always minded Yudhisthira, their oldest brother, and they all were devoted to their parents. They studied the sacred texts together and learned the basic skills of hunting and self-defense. They were respectful of and obedient to their parents and tutors.

In a few years, however, both King Pandu and Queen Madri died. Kunti and her children had to leave their forest home and went to live in the palace of Hastinapur. Dhritrashtra hated having his nephews in court, especially Yudhisthira, who as eldest stood to inherit the throne. Prince Duryodhana, of course, detested his five cousins and hated the fact that Grandfather Bhishma was fond of the Pandavas. Queen Gandhari's cunning brother, Shakuni, fanned the flames of hatred and jealousy in his nephew Duryodhana's heart, encouraging his greed and envy. "Forget the Pandavas. Just listen to me," he told Duryodhana. "You should be king! And your mother should take her rightful place as queen mother!" Duryodhana constantly squabbled with his cousins, and fights broke out regularly. It was certainly a good thing that the Pandava brothers were well trained in the arts of self-defense!

The sages, Kripa and Drona, were in charge of educating both the Pandavas and the Kauravas. They soon noted that the Pandavas were gifted with divine abilities. Arjuna, in particular, excelled as an archer. Impressed with Arjuna's passion for archery, Drona decided to test the boy's ability. He tied a clay bird to a tree and then said to all the boys, "You must shoot the bird's eye. But first, tell me what you see." "I see branches," said one boy. "I see leaves," said another. "We see the bird's tail and feathers," said several boys at once.

Drona asked Arjuna, "And what do you see?" Arjuna answered, "I see only the bird's eye." With a single graceful motion, he selected the thinnest arrow from his quiver and aimed. The arrow flew effortlessly to the exact middle of the bird's eye. The brothers and cousins gasped in astonishment.

"Well done," said Guru Drona.

Grandfather Bhishma also noted that Arjuna was quite different from all the other princes. He was kind and gentle, though he was born to be a warrior who would vanquish evil. As the son of the river goddess Ganga and Shantanu, the former king of Hastinapur, Bhishma was half human and half divine and had spent his childhood in Heaven. He could foresee the future, and he knew that the forces of evil were building on Earth. Bhishma had vowed in his youth that he would never inherit the throne, would never marry, and would never produce an heir. He had also vowed to selflessly and faithfully serve the throne of Hastinapur, whoever was the king. He had not considered the possibility that someone as greedy as Dhritrashtra would be king one day, or that he would groom his nasty son Duryodhana as crown prince.

Now as grandfather to both the Pandavas and the Kauravas, Bhishma could see into the hearts and minds of those around him. He knew that Yudhisthira, the eldest of the Pandava brothers, would rule with justice. But he also knew that Duryodhana would do anything within his power to be the next king. He would even kill members of his own family! Bhishma grew very fond of the Pandavas and took particular interest in grooming Arjuna, who would play a defining role in the war of good versus evil. Having received a number of powerful sacred weapons as gifts from his heavenly home, Bhishma took pains to teach Arjuna how to use them.

Bhishma worried about the future of Hastinapur. With his divine vision he could see that stage would soon be set for a war that would pit cousin against cousin, brother against brother, friend against friend. On one side would be Duryodhana and his cronies, and on the other side the Pandava brothers. Karna, Kunti's first born son, would take Duryodhana's side. Krishna (who was really Lord Vishnu, God of Preservation) had been born on Earth years before to rid the world of demons. He would be fighting alongside the Pandavas—his earthly father, Vasudeva, was Queen Kunti's brother, which made him their cousin. Uncle Vidur and the sages Drona and Kripa would get caught up in the conflict as well. Like all wars, this war would be complicated, and for complicated reasons, many good people—including Grandfather Bhishma—would find themselves fighting on the side of evil.

While rivalry among the cousins was unfolding in the palace of Hastinapur, Karna was growing up as an only child in the humble home of his adoptive parents. He showed great promise as an archer. He grew tall and strong and handsome and he glowed with an inner beauty. Among his many fine qualities, perhaps the most outstanding was his unparalleled generosity. At his daily midday worship of the sun, he focused his prayers on the act of giving. He was known far and wide as the one who would give the shirt off his own back, without hesitation and without a second thought.

Radha and Adhiratha adored their handsome, generous son. Radha showered him with affection. When he ran into the house after playing with his bow and arrows in the yard, she would scoop him up in her arms, mud and all, saying, "I love you, I love you, I *love* you!" And Karna would bury his face in her lap happily and say, "I love you, too, Mother."

Adhiratha was a kind and patient father who hoped to teach his son the art of training horses. But Karna had no interest in this trade. "Please, Father," he would say, "I want to be an archer." The little boy would hold up his beloved bow and arrows and smile his winning smile. "I want to be the greatest archer in the whole wide world!"

As it turned out, this was more than a mere boyhood fantasy. Karna had a recurrent dream that reflected his future as well as his past. In this dream he would see a basket floating in a river. Downstream, the water turned into blood. Bodies lay scattered about. Karna would try to run, but he would find himself unable to move. When he awoke, he would be drenched in sweat, his heart pounding. One day he told his mother about the dream. She was silent for a moment. Then she drew him close.

"Dearest son," she began. "You are old enough to know how you came to us." She told him the whole story. She explained how much they had yearned for children, how Adhiratha had found him floating in the river in a basket, and how all they could say at first was "Oh! Oh! Oh!" because they could not find words to express their joy. She said, "You were wrapped in soft silk and wore the gold earrings and shield that you still wear. We thought maybe your mother was a princess who, for some reason, could not raise you and had to let you go. May the gods bless her; she gave us a son."

Radha kissed Karna and put her arms around him. She continued, "That is what the basket means. But I am not sure what the rest of your dream is about. Perhaps it shows that war is filled with bloodshed and violence. You seem to be drawn to the life of a warrior, but we hope you will choose the path of peace and learn your father's trade instead. We will not hold you back though. You must follow your heart. You know we will love you always, whatever you decide." Karna hugged her tight. "Thank you," he said.

His parents' love indeed gave Karna the courage to follow his heart, and when he was old enough, he left home to seek out Sage Parashuram, who was known far and wide as the very best archery teacher. Karma knew that Sage Parasuram's school accepted only students of the Brahmin caste, but so strong was his ambition to learn archery that he chose to masquerade as a Brahmin lad to gain admittance. Karna had no way of knowing who his birth parents were, but he did know that his adoptive father was a tradesman, certainly not a Brahmin. Nevertheless, he presented himself to Sage Parasuram in a white dhoti and shawl, taking care to cover his golden shield. He had shaved his head, leaving nothing but a thin tuft of hair at the very top, and looked just like a young Brahmin boy ready to start training for the priesthood, the profession most Brahmins practiced.

Sage Parasuram never suspected that such a fine boy would lie about his background, and readily took him on as his student. Karna spent many years learning everything his teacher had to offer. One afternoon as the old Sage was taking a nap, resting his head on Karna's lap, a ghastly flesh-eating bug with enormous pincers landed on Karna's thigh. It tore a deep wound in the boy's flesh, and blood gushed down his leg.

Karna sat quietly through this ordeal. Generous as always, his first thought was for his teacher. He did not want to disturb his nap. But Sage Parasuram awoke anyway and saw the ragged, gaping wound. *Who could withstand such pain?* the sage thought suddenly. *Only a born warrior, someone of the Kashatriya caste!*

He sat up abruptly. "Tell the truth, Karna. Who are you?"

Karna knew it was useless to pretend any longer. He told the teacher all he knew about his past.

The sage was angry and hurt. "I have loved you and trusted you," he said. "You are the finest archer I have ever taught. But for years you have chosen to deceive me." Karna bowed his head as the sage continued. "As a consequence of your lies, when you most need them, you will forget the lessons you have learned through your deceit." Turning away sadly, Sage Parasuram dismissed his beloved student. "Go away. Leave this place forever."

Heartbroken, Karna roamed the countryside. He felt completely lost. He continued with his daily practice of archery, but carelessly and without taking proper aim. One day, his arrow struck a little calf in a nearby field. The calf belonged to a poor Brahmin, who stumbled through the woods to find Karna sitting on a rock, completely unaware of what had happened.

"You have killed my calf!" the Brahmin cried in anguish. "My sacred calf, my only source of livelihood! You have left me trapped in poverty!" The poor Brahmin shook his fist at Karna as he cursed him. "May a time come when you are trapped as well. May you find yourself unable to budge—unable to lift a finger to save your own life!"

Karna offered to pay for the calf; he offered to buy the man another; he offered to work to make up for the loss. Again and again he said how sorry he was. But nothing comforted the Brahmin's grief or calmed his rage. "Get out of my sight, you cursed man!" he shouted.

I am indeed a cursed man! Karna thought. *First I earn the wrath of my teacher, and now this poor Brahmin curses me.* Deeply unhappy, he wandered the land like a leaf caught in the wind, with no idea where to turn or what to do next.

One day, months later, Karna heard news of an archery tournament, and for the first time since his teacher dismissed him, he felt a glimmer of hope. The princes of Hastinapur had graduated from Sage Drona's school and were planning to display their skills to their citizens. Sage Drona had vowed that Arjuna would be named the best archer in the world. *There can't be two best archers. It is either him or me!* thought Karna, and with renewed determination he headed off to challenge Arjuna.

In Hastinapur lavish preparations had been made. There was a huge stadium for thousands of spectators, and vast arenas for the competitors. The citizens vied with each other for the best seats. The royal family was seated under a bright and colorful tent.

One by one the princes showed off their skills. There were sword fights, wrestling, chariot races, horse races, and elephant battles. Karna sat patiently. Finally Arjuna was announced: "The greatest archer in the world!" Arjuna showed absolute command. Not one arrow missed its mark. Not once did he hesitate or retake a shot. He was perfect. Amid the applause, Karna stood up, his figure tall and proud, his gold earrings and shield gleaming in the sun as he walked into the arena. Every face turned to stare at this unknown challenger. A hush fell over the crowd. "There can be only one greatest archer in the world," Karna shouted. "Let it be decided now." His first arrow brought down a torrent of rain. With the second arrow the rain ceased. He shot an arrow that burst into flames, then aimed another to extinguish them. He drew his bow and then vanished, only to reappear at the other end of the stadium. The stunned public broke into thunderous cheers.

Karna aimed his next arrow straight at Arjuna. "You must fight me, Arjuna, or accept that I am the greatest archer in the world."

The sun shone brightly, and Karna's golden ornaments were visible for miles. Kunti was watching from the royal tent, and when she saw the glint of reflected light, she realized who the challenger must be. Her heart brimmed with joy and relief to see Karna alive and well. But she was terrified to see her two sons preparing to do battle with each other. The powerful mix of emotions overwhelmed her. She fainted and was carried back to the palace.

In the meantime, Sage Kripa intervened. "Princes of Hastinapur only accept challenges from other princes. What kingdom and what ruling family do you represent?"

Karna stood silently. What could he say? His father was a charioteer. He had no way of knowing whether he had royal blood. The crowd began to jeer. "A commoner, a commoner!"

Duryodhana saw an opportunity. *An enemy of my enemy could be my friend,* he thought. Perhaps he could use Karna's skill and valor to defeat the Pandava brothers. Then he could inherit the throne! Duryodhana stood up and announced, "Here and now, I offer this fine archer the kingdom of Anga. As its king, he can compete against Arjuna." An amazed crowd fell silent again. What a turn of events! Karna had won—and then he had been disqualified—and now he was being made a king! What would happen next?

"How can I ever repay you?" Karna asked Duryodhana after receiving his crown.

"With everlasting friendship and loyalty," said Duryodhana.

"They are yours," said Karna without hesitation.

Adhiratha was also among the spectators. He, too, had recognized Karna from afar and rushed over to see what was happening. Karna rose from his new royal throne and ran to embrace him, saying, "Dear Father, I seek your blessings." Tears of pride and happiness streamed down Adhiratha's face.

However, it was decided that since Karna was not of royal blood (at least not as far as anyone knew) Arjuna could not accept his challenge. At the end of the day, the princes returned to their palaces and the citizens returned to their homes. Nevertheless, much had changed for everyone, and the balance of power in the world had shifted in favor of the wicked Duryodhana.

Duryodhana grew more envious, greedier, and meaner with each passing year. "How can get rid of my cousins forever?" he asked his nasty uncle Shakuni.

"We will trick them. We'll build a beautiful palace for them with graceful turrets and gleaming walls. They won't know that it is made of wax!" Shakuni answered with a crafty grin. "When they are asleep, we'll set the palace on fire!"

This trick might have worked, if not for Uncle Vidur, who had overheard their conversation. He told the builder to dig a secret tunnel that would lead to the outside and to make clay statues of five men and a woman—one for each bedroom. Vidur welcomed Kunti and her five sons into the new palace. Before leaving them, he turned to the brothers, saying casually, "By the way, I never told you how much I love mice. How smart they are! They travel in underground tunnels!" This odd revelation was a puzzle. What was Uncle Vidur talking about? Nevertheless, the Pandavas were courteous. "Yes," they agreed politely. "Mice are very sweet."

In the middle of the night, Shakuni's henchmen set fire to the palace. It was totally destroyed and all that was left was a huge pile of ashes and wax and the charred remains of six life-size figures— five men and one woman.

"Oh how sad!" Duryodhana declared, barely able to hide his smirk of satisfaction, "They all died! We must have a royal funeral for the unfortunate family." Little did he know that Bhima had woken up with the smell of acrid smoke and remembered Vidur's mysterious comment about mice and tunnels. *So that's what he meant,* thought Bhima. He picked up his four brothers and mother, Kunti, carrying them on his back as if they were mere feathers. He ran with them through the tunnel, away from the burning palace, all the way to the shores of River Ganga.

The family was relieved to have escaped the raging inferno, but the Pandava brothers were not born yesterday. They suspected Duryodhana and guessed that the fire was no mere accident. "I think he will try again," Bhima said. And so the newly homeless family decided to live in the forest while they figured out what to do next.

Although Duryodhana was sure that his cousins had perished, there were others who were equally sure that they had survived. For example, King Dhrupad knew they were alive. He admired the Pandava brothers greatly—in fact, he hoped that his beautiful daughter Draupadi would one day marry Arjuna, the archer par excellence he'd heard so much about. He announced an archery contest, knowing that the Pandava brothers would attend.

The task he set was next to impossible. It required lifting a bow that weighed a ton, shooting through a tiny hole in a plate overhead, aiming at a fish that hung from a pole, and hitting the exact center of the fish's eye. Furthermore, the archer could not actually see the fish, but rather only its reflection in a tub of water below. King Dhrupad knew of only one person who could accomplish such a feat. And indeed, Arjuna performed with customary ease and won Draupadi's hand in marriage. Draupadi was thrilled to marry Arjuna. In fact, with Kunti's permission, she ended up marrying all five brothers!

This news reached Duryodhana. "My cousins survived the fire! What shall I do now?" he asked Shakuni. "Invite them to Hastinapur," Shakuni said. "I will destroy them once and for all." Karna, pledged in loyalty to Duryodhana, said, "Challenge them in battle. I will help you win." But wise Grandfather Bhishma did not like these ideas. "War is not the answer," he said. "It will only end in tragedy. Duryodhana, you are just too greedy. Do the right thing! Split the kingdom in two and give one half to the Pandavas. It is their birthright." Uncle Vidur and Sage Drona echoed Bhishma, saying, "War is not the answer."

Uncle Vidur summoned the Pandava brothers to Hastinapur to propose division of the kingdom. So, in a grand procession, they set off for the palace with their new bride, Draupadi. King Dhrupad had provided a lavish dowry. There were elephants with gold-plated tusks, golden chariots covered with precious gems, an army of warriors on their prancing horses, countless servants carrying rosewood chests filled with diamonds and pearls, silks and fine leathers. There were cattle with cowherds to care for them. There were chairs and beds and sofas and tables, pots and pans and knives and forks, and all kinds of delicious delicacies. "I know you will love Draupadi more than life itself," King Dhrupad had said as he gave away his daughter in marriage. "We will," said the Pandava brothers. Amid joyous beating of drums, their royal entourage made its way to Hastinapur.

When they arrived, Dhritrashtra told Yudhisthira of the plan to

divide the kingdom. "It's the right thing to do," he said. "It's only fair that Duryodhana stays here, since he is used to it now, and you will be king of Khandava Prastha! It is a huge region! You can use your rich dowry to build a palace! Everybody will be happy!"

In fact, Khandava Prastha was a hostile place, barren and gloomy and unfit for human habitation. Arjuna worried to himself, *How can I bring my lovely wife to such a desolate place?* Lord Indra saw his distress and ordered the architect of Heaven to build a beautiful city for his son. "Make it as wonderful as Heaven," he said. The city was called Indraprastha in honor of Indra, and it transformed the desolate region into a lively and beautiful place, filled with art and music and
all the comforts of living,
just like Heaven.

Yudhisthira was a good and just ruler, and his subjects prospered. As a gift for the noble young king, Krishna asked one of his demons to build an auditorium in the city center. Delighted, the demon unleashed his creative genius and soon the auditorium attracted tourists from far and wide—including Duryodhana. He turned green with envy on seeing such opulence and beauty. The main hall was adorned with gold-plated pillars. Sunlight streamed through stained-glass windows, while cool, flower-scented breezes wafted from the exquisite gardens and through the corridors. Ornate domes formed the skyline.

Duryodhana came upon a section of flooring that looked like a shimmering pool of water. He gathered his robes and stepped carefully, and then realized that it was actually a floor of translucent quartz. When he came across another similarly shining floor, he walked on carelessly, assuming it was an illusion. But this time the shimmering really was water. He slipped and fell, drenching his royal robes. Duryodhana was the unfortunate kind of person who could never laugh at himself, and he was furious when he heard Draupadi giggle innocently at his mistake. He returned to his father in rage. "This is not what we'd planned!" he complained. "My cousins are rich and famous. I have been insulted! Draupadi made a mockery of me!"

"I know what to do," said the wily Shakuni. "Invite them for a game of dice. I'll play on your behalf. I *always* win," he said with a sneering laugh. "And then, when they lose, you can banish them from the kingdom." "Yes!" said Duryodhana enthusiastically. But Uncle Vidur and Grandfather Bhishma protested, "Shakuni, you are a shameless cheater! This is a dishonorable plan!" Nevertheless,

Dhritrashtra supported his son. "If it will make you happy . . . ," he said, and he sent an invitation to the Pandavas.

The brothers didn't imagine that Shakuni would resort to foul play. Yudhisthira played against Shakuni. In one game, he lost his riches. In the next roll, he lost his palace. He lost his land, his city, his kingdom; he even lost his crown. He couldn't believe his bad luck. He raised his bet, desperately hoping to win back his kingdom, and rolling the dice again, he lost his brothers. He lost Draupadi.

Yudhisthira had been cheated out of everything. Everything he owned and loved now belonged to Duryodhana.

Greedy Duryodhana was ecstatic, "Go back to the forest where you belong," he said. "Be gone for twelve years. If I find you in the thirteenth year, I will banish you for another thirteen years. You are all my slaves and must obey!"

The Pandava brothers were born and raised in the forest. Survival was no problem for them, and they spent their time meditating on what to do next. Although they did not wish to fight their cousins and uncles and grandfather, they came to understand that there was no other way. Still, this was a difficult choice, especially for the gentle warrior Arjuna. He felt it would break his heart to battle his kith and kin, even the evil Duryodhana and his cronies. He roamed the forest, praying to Shiva, Lord of Destruction. He fasted, practiced the most difficult yoga positions for hours in penance, his hair matted, his face gaunt. "How can I kill my own relatives? War is not the answer. But peace is not possible. How can I best follow dharma?" His mind went in circles, his heart was tormented.

Shiva heard his lamentations and appeared in a hunter's attire just as a demon disguised as a wild boar attacked Arjuna. Shiva and Arjuna both shot their arrow at the same time. "There is only one way to find out whose arrow killed the wild boar," the hunter said. "Let us see who is the better archer. Shoot me."

Arjuna aimed with precision, but miraculously the hunter dodged every arrow. Arjuna was shocked—he had never before missed his mark. Then the hunter shot his arrow, and in an instant, Arjuna found himself bleeding on the ground. Humbly, he called to Shiva, offering flowers and prayers. When he looked up, he was astonished to see the flowers were now on the head of the hunter! Another miracle! Arjuna recognized Shiva and bowed. Delighted with the young man's humility and offerings, Shiva, who knew that the coming war was inevitable, offered Arjuna divine weapons in return. He gave strict instructions. "This one is Pashupatastra," he said, handing Arjuna a shining crescent-shaped arrow. "It can destroy the entire world. You must use it only as a last resort." Then he presented a massive bow and arrow. "This is Gandeeva. It will destroy demons and evil spirits."

"Thank you," said Arjuna.

"And now I will take you to your father Indra. Look! His chariot is already here!" Shiva pointed to a chariot drawn by ten thousand white horses, racing across the sky like a shooting star.

This was truly a magical day for Arjuna. In a flash, he was in Heaven, meeting his father, Indra, God of Thunder and Lightning. Indra presented him with another special weapon, giving his own strict instructions. "Use this when you need my help, and I will send thunderbolts and hail and thick clouds to darken the sky. Your enemy will be blinded by my storm."

"Thank you," said Arjuna, once again.

During their twelve years of life in the forest, the Pandava brothers received many more weapons and divine gifts from the gods. After spending one year in complete disguise, they returned to Hastinapur—alive and well. But Duryodhana still refused to give them back their land and wealth.

Krishna knew how the Pandava brothers had been cheated out of their land, and he decided to step in. Born on Earth as Queen Kunti's nephew, he was allowed to address the royal court, where he tried to convince Duryodhana to relent. But even when the god himself intervened, Duryodhana refused. "Never," he said, "I will not give them land equal to the tip of a needle!"

"I came as an ambassador of peace," said Krishna. "But I see that war will be the only way to bring justice." He glared at the courtiers. "You are allowing cheaters and tricksters to rule the land. The Pandava brothers will avenge the injustice done to them."

King Dhritrashtra began to worry. "Are my nephews going to fight us," he asked his wise brother Vidur. "Of course they are," Vidur answered. "They will fight for their birthright. You must make peace and give them back their land." But Dhritrashtra had never been able to refuse his son's dark desires. "I cannot ask Duryodhana to give back his winnings," he said.

Bhishma and Vidur and Krishna pleaded with Duryodhana. "If you don't give back the land you have stolen," said Krishna, "war is inevitable." You are too greedy. You're breaking all the laws of Heaven." But Duryodhana was unmoved. Instead, the nasty fellow summoned the palace guards. "Arrest that man! He does not belong here!" he said, pointing at Krishna. The entire court was stunned when, in Krishna's place, Lord Vishnu appeared in all his glory with Brahma, God of Creation, on his forehead and Shiva, God of Destruction, on his chest. "Arrest me if you dare," Krishna challenged, but the wicked prince had already fainted in fright.

Later that night, both Arjuna and Duryodhana approached Krishna as he lay sleeping. They both wanted to ask for his help. Duryodhana stood by the headboard, glaring down at the divine being. Arjuna knelt at Krishna's feet with humility.

Krishna awoke and spoke to Arjuna. "Tell me what you need," he said.

Duryodhana interrupted rudely, saying, "Me! You must help me first! Give me your army!"

"I saw you first, Arjuna. What do you need?" Krishna asked Arjuna again.

"Nothing but you," Arjuna said simply.

"Then I will be your charioteer. Duryodhana, you may have my army," Krishna said.

Hah! thought Duryodhana. *I have won again against the Pandavas!* He appointed Grandfather Bhishma as his commander in chief. Bhishma agreed reluctantly. "I do not wish to fight my grandsons, but I will. I am bound by my vow to serve the king of Hastinapur without question," he said sadly.

The day before the war began, Arjuna asked Krishna to park their chariot between the two armies so he could inspect the armed forces on both sides. Arjuna saw Grandfather Bhishma, Uncle Vidur, Sage Drona, his cousins, relatives, and friends on Duryodhana's side, and his eyes filled with tears. He turned to Krishna, his divine charioteer. "I can't do this," he said. "I don't want to fight my old friends and relatives. No kingdom is worth so many lives, so much bloodshed."

Krishna recognized Arjuna's confusion and despair. "Arjuna," he began, "this is your destiny. Put aside your personal concerns and feelings and place yourself instead in the hands of the gods. You were born to be a warrior, destined to fight on the side of good. You are the instrument through which the Divine will work its plan." Krishna pointed across the war field and said, "Duryodhana is cruel and greedy. He will stop at nothing to get his own way. He stole from you and your brothers. He tried to kill you many times. You must not let him win this time. You have no choice but to do your duty and fight him. You must follow the law of dharma."

As he spoke, Krishna took on an immense and endless form—the whole universe, radiant and eternal, the blazing cosmos, the spirit that encompasses all. Arjuna was overwhelmed with awe, filled with wonder. His doubts and fears now seemed tiny in comparison with the amazing spirit that appeared before him. "Now I understand. You are the divine being who is everywhere, all at once, and in everything. Thank you for your words of wisdom. You are with me and I am afraid no more. Filled with courage, Arjuna picked up his bow and arrows. "Let us go," he said to Krishna.

In the meantime, a few days before the war, Sun saw bad omens and feared for his son Karna's life. He visited Karna in a dream and said, "Son, beware. Lord Indra will visit you disguised as a Brahmin. He will ask you for the golden earrings and shield I gave you when you were just born. Your mother knows that these charms keep you safe. If you give them away, you will die. My son, beware. Do not give them away." As Karna stirred, the dream ended. The fragments that he could remember in the morning puzzled him. He thought, *Why would Sun call me "my son"? Who is the woman that Sun called "your mother"?*

The next day at noon, during his midday worship, Karna noticed something strange. The sun shone brightly in a cloudless sky, but he heard thunder in the distance. *Ah, he thought, Sun and Indra are trying to outdo each other!* Something stirred in his memory— was this part of his dream? Then he heard another rumble of thunder and looked around. A Brahmin was approaching.

"Please," said the man, "would you give me your earrings and your shield?"

"Of course," said Karna, generous as always. "They are yours." Heedless of the warning he had received from Sun in his dream the night before, with his knife he cut off the earrings and cut away the golden shield, leaving raw, bleeding wounds in their place.

"I admire your courage and generosity," said Indra—for indeed the Brahmin was Indra. As he ran his fingers over Karna's gaping wounds, the skin healed without a trace of scarring, flawless and radiant as before. "Accept this gift, my weapon, Indrastra, in return," Indra continued. "You may use it once. If you miss your target, the weapon will come back to me. Aim well, and your enemy will surely die." With these words, he held out a long, gleaming spear.

"Thank you, my Lord," Karna said and bowed his head in greeting and recognition. When he looked up again, the Brahmin was gone.

Karna soon received another visit from the gods. Lord Krishna had discovered Kunti's secret long before, and knew that Karna was her firstborn son. After his efforts toward peace at Hastinapur failed, he approached Karna. "No one can escape this war, but you can choose your side. Side with the Pandava brothers. They are good men. Leave Duryodhana, who is a greedy despot. Fight on the side of justice."

"I will not leave my dear friend at his time of greatest need," Karna answered. "When everyone at the stadium jeered me, he offered his support and embraced me warmly. The Pandavas insult me and sneer at my birth. Duryodhana respects me for my skills. For all his evil acts, he is my friend." Karna's voice grew passionate. "I will not deceive a friend—neither from fear, nor temptation, nor coaxing. I would rather die." Lord Krishna heard the resolve in Karna's voice and knew it would be pointless to push him further.

Queen Kunti, too, attempted to convince Karna to leave Duryodhana. She knew that Duryodhana would use Karna in an effort to destroy her five sons. She also knew that without Karna, Duryodhana would not have the courage to go to war. And she couldn't bear the thought of her sons battling one another. *It is time to tell Karna about his birth. Surely, truth will sway him,* she thought. She approached Karna just as he was completing his midday meditation.

"What can I do for you, Queen Kunti?" Karna asked.

Kunti took a deep breath and began, "You must call me 'Mother,'" she said. "I was barely twelve years old when Sun, your father, gave you to me, and I hadn't seen you again until the archery contest. But I recognized you in the stadium. Even as a newborn babe, you wore the golden earrings and shield that Sun had given you." Her voice began to shake, but she steadied herself. "Dear son, you must try to understand. I was so young when you were born to me! I was so afraid! I had to send you away, but I tried my best to send you safely." She reached out and put her hand on Karna's shoulder. "My son, please join the Pandava princes. You must not fight your own brothers. They will welcome you as their older brother. Duryodhana is a bad man. I do not want any of my sons to die . . ." Kunti's voice trailed off into a soft sob.

Thus Karna finally learned who his birth parents were. For years and years he had wondered. He thought, *How strange, now that I know, the truth makes little difference.* "Thank you, Queen Kunti," he said formally.

Kunti said again, "Please call me 'Mother.'"

"No" said Karna. "I cannot. "You, too, must try to understand. When I was hungry and needed mother's milk, it was not you who fed me. When I got hurt, it was not you who kissed my cuts and bruises. When I had nightmares, it was not you who comforted me. When I was mocked and jeered at the stadium, it was not you who claimed me. It was not you who ran to embrace me."

"But I couldn't. I had fainted." Kunti tried to explain, tried to excuse herself, but Karna cut her off.

"You say that you are my mother. No. My mother is Radha, and for all her poverty, she outshines any royalty or riches. You tell me that Sun is my father. But the sun pales in greatness next to my father, the humble Adhiratha. They are the parents who took me in when I was homeless and abandoned, who raised me and cared for me. You, Queen Kunti, are the one who cast me away."

Karna and Kunti were both sobbing now. For an instant they embraced as mother and son—and then just as quickly they released each other. There was a chasm between them that only time might bridge. But time was the one thing they did not have.

"Queen Kunti, how can you, of all people, ask me to abandon a friend?" asked Karna. "But I cannot refuse anyone," he continued with a bitter smile. "I will honor your request. You want your sons to survive. My enmity is only with Arjuna. If I kill him, or if he kills me, you will still have five sons as before. I promise not to kill your other four sons."

Kunti left with a sad heart. It was too late to prevent this terrible war. Karna's heart was heavy also. For him, too, the war loomed darkly. He could not bring himself to abandon a friend, as he himself had once been abandoned. He knew, though, that the coming war would pitch good against evil. Through loyalty to Duryodhana, he was pledged to the wrong side. Deep in his heart, Karna understood that he himself must die so that good might prevail. He would fight hard, but he would lose. He walked slowly away. He knew each step took him closer to his own death.

The Mahabharata war was fierce and intense, lasting just eighteen days. As Arjuna had feared, there was much bloodshed and death. Many brave warriors died on both sides. Grandfather Bhishma fought valiantly for Duryodhana, honoring his old vow to support the king of Hastinapur. Finally, when he lay mortally wounded in a hail of arrows, the Pandava brothers came to pay him their respects. Arjuna drove a spear into the ground so that sacred River Ganga, Bhishma's mother, could rise in a fountain to shower him with soft, cool water as he lay dying.

With Bhishma's death, Karna rose to the rank of Duryodhana's commander in chief. He had long waited for a chance to kill his rival, Arjuna, and prove himself the finest archer on Earth. His only worry was the loss of his golden shield and earrings. He had the powerful weapon, Indrastra, but he could use it only once. He'd saved it for Arjuna.

But just as Arjuna's destiny was to prevail on the side of good, Karna's destiny was to die because he had sided with evil. On the eighteenth day of battle, when Karna saw a chance to hurl the Indrastra at Arjuna, Indra immediately shrouded the sun with dark storm clouds. Karna may have hesitated just a second in the sudden darkness, but his aim was impeccable and the spear would have killed Arjuna in an instant. Krishna, however, saw it coming, and shifted his weight at just the right moment, tipping the chariot so that the spear sliced off the top of Arjuna's crown, leaving Arjuna unscathed. Karna had lost his opportunity. The Indrastra returned in a flash to the heavens, as Indra had said it would.

Karna's luck was truly running out. The wheels of his chariot sunk into the deep mud of the battlefield. Karna jumped down and tried to pry the wheels loose, but they refused to budge. He was trapped, just as the old Brahmin had foretold. He tried to send an arrow toward Arjuna, but suddenly he could not remember how to use his bow, just as Sage Parasuram had predicted.

Lord Krishna signaled quickly to Arjuna, "Now! It's your only opportunity! Shoot!" Arjuna took aim and Karna didn't have a chance. His earrings and shield would have protected him, but, generous to a fault, he had given those away to Indra.

Karna's death tipped the balance of power to the Pandavas. Duryodhana's army was large and powerful, but the Pandavas were united and determined in their fight against evil. They knew their cause was just, and they had on their side the power of good and the support of the gods.

Karna's last thoughts were for Radha and Adhiratha, his beloved parents. The generous Karna, though he had made fatal choices, had truly lived for giving. He gave his life, his final gift, out of loyalty and love. Because of this sacrifice, Karna traveled easily from this world to the next. His journey was blessed and watched over by Lord Krishna. Although Arjuna had won the batle, he knew that without Krishna's help, he could not have killed Karna. He bowed to Karna and acknowledged, "Karna, you are indeed the greatest archer in the whole wide world."

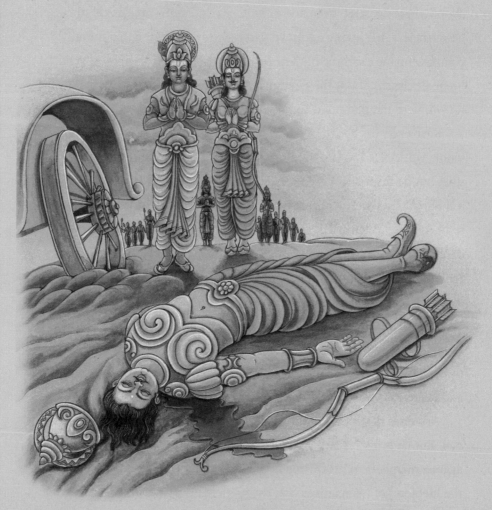

A Note to Parents and Teachers

The Mahabharata describes the inner struggles that people experience when they try to understand their real purpose in life. In India, this purpose is known as a person's dharma—his or her divine destiny.

Karna, abandoned by his mother at birth, finds himself at a disadvantage as he tries to understand his place in the world. His is the story of many children who have been adopted—he loves his adoptive parents, but all his life he wonders about his birth parents and about where he came from and how he arrived at his childhood home. Nevertheless, his loving adoptive parents provide him with a moral compass by the example of their own steadfast devotion to him. When he finally learns about the circumstances of his birth, his love and loyalty remain with the parents who took him in and raised him.

Karna sets his eye on the coveted title of being the best archer in the whole world. He has the training, devotion, bravery, and skill to win this title, but he resorts to deceit and lies to achieve his goal. By posing as a Brahmin student, he cheats his teacher. This flaw brings Karna closer to his demise. Even when he learns that the Pandava princes are his own brothers—and that by joining hands with them he could live—he remains loyal to his friend Duryodhana. By the moral code explained in the Mahabharata, this last act of selfless loyalty is the only honorable choice for Karna. By giving his life, and by giving up his ambition to be known as the best archer in the world, Karna allows the forces of good to prevail. To the end, Karna remains true to his personal code of honor and keeps his vow of generosity and charity.

Arjuna is destined to be a warrior who will help defeat the forces of evil. But he is a kind and gentle soul; he does not want to fight a war against members of his own family. For him, no earthly riches are worth the lifeblood of his relatives. On the battlefield, he is torn between what he wants to do and what he must do because it is his duty. Arjuna's inner struggle is experienced, to a greater or lesser degree, by other characters in this epic as well. Grandfather Bhishma, Uncle Vidur, and the sages Drona and Kripa, must all honor family ties or promises and vows made in the past by fighting on the side of the evil Duryodhana. But in their heart of hearts, they wish they could side with the Pandavas, who represent the forces of good. Like Karna, they must give up their own lives to let good defeat evil.

Though circumstances allow Arjuna to win the war against evil and to be known as the best archer in the whole world, he is aware that none of this could have happened without Krishna's help. He realizes the limits of his own abilities, and—in true humility—recognizes the greatness of his arch enemy, Karna, declaring him to be the best archer in the whole wide world.

But the grand Mahabharata epic is not only about who wins what title. It is a narrative of the inner struggles people face when they find themselves in situations of which they cannot get out, situations that ask them to rise above themselves and stand up for their personal moral codes so that they may be able to fulfill their dharma—the true purpose of their lives.

About the Authors and the Artists

Vatsala Sperling, PhD, PDHom, RSHom (NA), CCH, a native of India, is fluent in Indian languages and Sanskrit. She learned these traditional stories at her mother's feet and enjoys introducing them to children of the Western world. Before marrying and moving to the United States, she was the Chief of Clinical Microbiological Services at the largest children's hospital in India, where she published extensively and conducted research with the World Health Organization, Denmark. Since moving to the United States, she studied homeopathy at Misha Norland's school and has established her own private practice of homeopathy both in Vermont and in Costa Rica. She is the author of the original eight books that now comprise this volume. She is also the author of *For Seven Lifetimes* and *The Ayurvedic Isolation Diet* (www.InnerTraditions.com) and several essays and papers based on her practice of homeopathy (www.Rochester homeopathy.com). She lives in Vermont with her husband and son.

Harish Johari (1934–1999) was a true Renaissance man. A successful author, gifted painter and sculptor, distinguished North Indian musician, composer, poet, gemologist, and Tantric scholar, he held degrees in philosophy and literature. Harish studied painting with Shri Chandra Bal and developed the Harish Johari Painting Tradition— the traditional style of Indian wash painting that is used in the illustrations for this book. In this volume, he illustrated "Ganga: The River That Flows from Heaven to Earth," with assistance from Pieter Weltevrede. Harish loved teaching Indian traditions to Western students and was the original inspiration for this collection of traditional Indian stories for Western children. His other books include *The Monkeys and the Mango Tree, Spiritual Traditions of India Coloring Book, The Yoga of Snakes and Arrows, Chakras, Tools for Tantra, Ayurvedic Healing Cuisine, Ayurvedic Massage, Numerology, Dhanwantari, The Healing Power of Gemstones,* and *Breath, Mind, and Consciousness.* He also produced several recordings of traditional Indian chants (www.InnerTraditions.com). His devoted international students have formed the Sanatan Society to promote his teachings, and more information about Harish can be found on their website (sanatansociety.com).

Pieter Weltevrede, a native of the Netherlands, is a social scientist by training, but his career took a dramatic turn when, in 1977, he began his artistic

studies with Harish Johari. Johari, a master artist and *jnana yogi*, made Pieter his primary art student and taught him the unique wash technique used in the illustrations for this book. Pieter has also studied with Shri Chandra Bal. Since beginning his artistic studies, he has spent part of every year studying in India to hone his artistic skills. In this volume he is the illustrator for "How Ganesh Got His Elephant Head," "How Parvati Won the Heart of Shiva," "Ram the Demon Slayer," and "The Magical Adventures of Krishna." He assisted Harish Johari with the illustrations for "Ganga," and assisted his son, Nona Weltevrede, with some of the illustrations for "Who Is the Greatest Archer in the World: Karna or Arjuna?" Today Pieter travels and presents workshops each year in Europe and the United States, when he is not busy painting in the Netherlands or in India. Pieter is a member of the Sanatan Society, an international networking association of students of the late Harish Johari, and a selection of Pieter's paintings in the Indian classical tradition can be viewed on the Sanatan Society website (sanatansociety.com). He is also the coauthor of *Awakening the Chakras*.

Sandeep Johari, a native of India, was raised by his uncle Harish Johari, who taught him classical Indian painting. He also studied painting with his uncle's teacher Shri Chandra Bal. Sandeep pursued a career as the creative director for an advertising agency in New Delhi, India, but he has more recently returned to classical Indian painting, producing an ambitious series of paintings on the monkey god Hanuman and many individual paintings of other Hindu deities. In this volume Sandeep illustrated "Hanuman's Journey to the Medicine Mountain" and did many of the illustrations for "Who Is the Greatest Archer in the World: Karna or Arjuna?" Sandeep is a member of the Sanatan Society, which was formed to honor his uncle Harish. More of Sandeep's artwork can be found on the Sanatan Society website (sanatansociety.com).

Nona Weltevrede got in touch with Indian culture at a young age by watching his father, Pieter Weltevrede, and his father's mentor, Harish Johari, paint. In this volume Nona did many of the illustrations for "Who Is the Greatest Archer in the World: Karna or Arjuna?" A graduate of the Dutch Academy of Art and Design, St. Joost, he lives in Buren, Holland.

About the Illustrations

The original illustrations in this book are wash paintings done in both watercolors and opaque tempera paints. The artists created each piece following a nine-step traditional Indian process.

1. First, using watercolors, the artist drew the outlines of everything in the painting.
2. Before filling in the outlines he had to "fix" the line drawing, pouring water over the painted surface until only the paint absorbed by the paper remained.
3. Once the paper was completely dry, he filled in all the forms with color, using three tones for each color to achieve a three-dimensional effect: highlight, middle tone, and depth.
4. Once again the colors had to be fixed by pouring water over the painting until the water ran off clear.
5. Then, still using watercolor, he applied the background colors.
6. Once again the colors had to be fixed.
7. Then the artist was ready to apply the wash, which is done with opaque tempera paints mixed to a consistency between thin honey and boiled milk. Before applying the wash, he had to wet the painting thoroughly, letting any excess water drip off. Then he applied the tempera paint until the whole painting appeared to be behind a colored fog. While the wash color was still wet, he took a dry brush and removed it from the face, hands, and feet of any figures. Then he let the wash dry completely.
8. Once again water had to be poured over the entire painting to fix the color. Many of the paintings received several washes and fixes before the right color tone was achieved. The wash color is important because it sets the emotional mood of the entire painting.
9. Finally, the artist went back in and redefined the delicate line work of the piece, outlining faces, fingers, toes, and ornaments with the depth color. These finishing touches allow the painting to reemerge from within the clouds of wash.